The Least of These

Kathleen Neely

The Least of These
COPYRIGHT 2019 by Kathleen Neely

Contact Information: titleadmin@pelicanbookgroup.com

All scripture quotations, unless otherwise indicated, are taken from the King James translation, public domain.

Cover Art by *Nicola Martinez*

Harbourlight Books, a division of Pelican Ventures, LLC
www.pelicanbookgroup.com PO Box 1738 *Aztec, NM * 87410

Harbourlight Books sail and mast logo is a trademark of Pelican Ventures, LLC

Publishing History
First Harbourlight Edition, 2019
Paperback Edition ISBN 978-1-5223-0194-3
Electronic Edition ISBN 978-1-5223-0193-6
Published in the United States of America

Dedication

To Brittney
"May you be blessed by the Lord, my daughter."
~Ruth 3:10

Prologue

Then the righteous will answer him, 'Lord, when did we see you hungry and feed you, or thirsty and give you something to drink? When did we see you a stranger and invite you in, or needing clothes and clothe you? When did we see you sick or in prison and go to visit you?'

The King will reply, 'Truly I tell you, whatever you did for one of the least of these brothers and sisters of mine, you did for me. ~Matthew 25:37-40 NIV

I sat bolt upright, not quite sure what had roused me. Did I hear voices and a slamming door downstairs or just imagine them?

The sirens screaming in the distance were real. The alarm clock glowed 4:15 AM. in neon red. I lay wide awake with no sleep left in me.

Climbing out of my bed, the November chill sent shivers down my arms. I inched the bedroom door open. Night sconces cast shadows in the darkened hallway, fingers of light reaching down the wall. Thick carpeting absorbed the noise of my steps. The sirens still shrieked their warning call somewhere far off. My stomach churned. I held my hand over it to ward off that sick feeling.

Lights on the first floor sent a softer glow up the stairway. Reaching Edwin's door, I rotated the knob. Light didn't penetrate into the dark room, but small fissures from the gap in the door confirmed an unused bed, still made from yesterday, neat and smooth, pillows plumped like Leticia always left them. How could he be out at 4:15 in the morning? My heart raced, my mind grabbing at any possible explanation. A choked sob arrived from below. I hurried toward the stairs. As I stepped down the wide, curved staircase, my hand gliding on the smooth, polished surface of a massive wood railing, Leticia appeared at the bottom.

"Go back to bed, Scott." Red eyes and a husky voice betrayed her as she climbed toward me.

"Where're my mom and dad?" Where was Edwin? Leticia touched my shoulders to turn me around and motion me back upstairs. I lay awake until daylight, my pulse racing, unable to still my trembling hands.

~*~

I didn't see my parents in the morning. They made poor Leticia break the news to me. How typical. The second person to tell me was the morning news anchor. After a cheerful "good morning" and a wide-angle shot of a brilliant fire-orange sunrise, he affixed a somber expression for the next segment on his scripted card.

"Edwin Harrington, sixteen-year-old son of the prominent defense attorney Charles Harrington, was found dead last night from an apparent overdose. A man from the night cleaning company discovered Harrington's body under the bleachers of the Ravenwood High School's football field."

I waited to hear my name. But he didn't know. He couldn't, because no one did. I took my secret and hid it deep inside my guilt.

1

Scott Harrington

The Tenth Street Bridge spanned overhead with a thousand metallic arms reaching skyward in the eerie darkness. It crossed the Monongahela River, connecting Pittsburgh to the South Side. The insufficient cardboard wouldn't hold my 6'2" frame, so I curled my knees close to my body to keep out the chill of touching cold concrete. Every joint throbbed. The acrid scent of puddled asphalt burned my nostrils.

I sat up and readjusted my backpack against the concrete pylon. Raindrops sparkled like diamonds in the glow of streetlamps, which also illuminated the other men. Three slept well, as evidenced by the heavy snoring. A drunken slumber, if the discarded bottles were any indication. About ten feet from where I sat, another man stretched flat on the icy cement, wide-eyed yet oblivious to anything around him. The dark of night swallowed the blackness of his face, but his large white eyes held a wild and unrelenting stare at the grating of the bridge above. Where had his trip taken him?

The fifth man appeared no older than a teenager. Wide awake, his gaze darted from side to side, nervousness cloaking him like a well-worn jacket.

Sandy-colored hair, shaggy and unkempt, escaped his steel-gray hoodie. No cardboard insulated him from the bite of the cold surface. A crumpled up sweatshirt served as his pillow. If it weren't three in the morning, I might have attempted a conversation. But voices at this hour would be an intrusion.

Tight fingers gripped a backpack bulging beyond the capacity of the zipper. Was he concerned that someone would take his belongings if he succumbed to sleep? Perhaps I was the naïve one. Maybe he watched to see when everyone else slept and pilfered what he could. Was that why his bag was overstuffed? I pulled my backpack closer and readjusted my head to protect it. It wasn't much, but it was mine.

Glancing in his direction, I took care to avoid eye contact. He looked like Richie Cunningham from *Happy Days*, a touch of red in the sandy-colored hair and a pale complexion. But he wasn't a clean-cut suburbanite kid with his own bedroom and a doting mother. Where were his parents? Wasn't there anyone he could turn to?

An occasional car infringed upon the night sounds as it rattled the trestle above. I closed my eyes, imagining I was somewhere else, someplace sleep would come. My childhood home, the pretentious estate with all the grandeur of old money. What would my father think if he could see me now? Those were memories I didn't care to visit. Much better to focus on my own little home, the comfortable living room, the smell of wood burning in the fireplace. A place where my mind could escape. Cozy and simple, the feet of my recliner raised as I sank into the soft brown leather, swallowing me with comfort. The TV hummed with a sportscaster's dialogue while I drifted into the shadows of my mind, almost forgetting I was lying on a thin piece of cardboard under a cold bridge.

The inclination to compare myself to others was a part of my nature I couldn't seem to overcome, and it could be exhausting. Charles Harrington made certain that I never forgot that I didn't measure up to Edwin. There was one brief moment when a flash of insight helped me understand. My father wielded it as a motivator. Nothing would have been enough, because then I might have stopped striving. It's hard to overcome a lifetime of indoctrination, so over time, that insight faded.

There were times when I thought I'd mastered the tendency to compare myself, when I was satisfied with who I'd become, but then I'd find myself in the company of someone whose accomplishments diminished mine or left me standing in the shadow of my father's censure.

The opposite was true on this night as I slept under a bridge for the first time. I fought the tendency to feel somewhat superior to the five men who shared this underpass. I came here to blend in, to assimilate into this culture, yet the egocentric part of me wanted to make sure everyone knew I didn't belong here. But that attitude would be a detriment. I needed to guard against it to accomplish anything.

Sometime before morning light, I slept. I woke to discover two of the snoring men still fast asleep, while the third relieved himself on the other side of the pylon. He paid no notice of me, finished his task, and disappeared into the hazy fog. The man with the wild eyes closed them in sleep. A bare stretch of concrete remained where Richie Cunningham with the hoodie had been. I checked to ensure that my backpack and blanket remained intact and found both secure.

Judging from the predawn light, it was around six o'clock so I'd gotten only two or three hours of sleep. Rising, my body was unbendable until I began to stretch the stiffness away and then blood flowed to my limbs again. Desperate for a bathroom and a hot cup of coffee, I began walking.

~*~

The yellow brick of St. John's Episcopal Church still held its original charm. It had graced this corner for over a hundred years, with beauty and architecture unparalleled by the new wave of nondescript churches. A white cross peeked down from the cupola, bidding all to come. Walking past the grand oaken doors, I tried to envisage what stood behind them, imagining rich maroon carpeting cushioning dark pews, all illuminated by the rainbow prisms from a thousand pieces of stained glass fashioned to depict the garden of Gethsemane and Jesus with the children.

Then it hit me. I envisioned the interior of my childhood church which, as teenagers, Edwin and I coined Fellowship of the Elite. Worshippers showing off their designer fashions and glittering jewels. How discordant would it be to visit a Sunday service dressed in these frayed jeans and in obvious need of a shower?

The doors to St. John's remained locked throughout the week. I walked the manicured path to the side of the church, breathing in the fragrance of fresh grass and withering flowers, a contrast to the stagnant scent of auto exhaust and concrete. A simple sign posted on the gray, metal door noted the hours for breakfast. They began serving at six. I prayed the door would open when I turned the knob, and it cooperated, the heavy metal scraping the surface of a frayed welcome mat. I entered the oversized room with its large industrial kitchen and the welcoming aroma of coffee.

A small portion of the space in the vast room had been set up with tables where pancakes were being served. People already occupied some seats, even at this early hour. Most of them scattered throughout the area with their coffee and pancakes, spaced for solitude. I needed human interaction. Scanning the tables, I chose one with two men and carried my cup and plate over to join them.

"Good morning." I sat down without asking permission. A grunt and a nod came from my left.

The man seated across the table rewarded me with a hearty welcome. "Howdie do." He flashed a grin as wide as his voice was loud. I glanced around as a few heads turned our way. "Always a good mornin' here. We get the best coffee and hotcakes in town. Name's Pete. This here's D.J." His attempted introduction brought another grunt.

Pete's grin revealed sparse and decaying teeth. Age spots peppered his arms, and red cheeks bookended a bulky, bulbous nose. His booming tones continued to reverberate throughout the room, oblivious to the fact that he displaced the quiet.

"Good to meet you, Pete. I'm Scott." I muffled my words hoping he'd get the message. "So Pete, anywhere else someone like me can get a meal around here? This ain't gonna last me 'til supper."

"No sir-ee, Scotty. That it ain't." His voice still

thundered. "Couple'a places you can try. If'n I were you, I'd head on down to Stanwix and try the shelter there. Or you can try Hope House. It's a place that lets a feller stay and tries to get him turned around, like learnin' new job stuff."

I knew about Hope House, but it wasn't what I needed. "So how does the Stanwix Street one work? I'm kinda new at this. A little down on my luck right now."

"Well, ain't we all." His eyes sparkled despite the bloodshot streaks. "Ain't we all. First time you go, you gotta tell 'em some stuff about you and sign a paper agreein' to their rules. After that, you just sign in when you go. You can get a good, hot meal and a bed for the night."

Right about now, a bed sounded like heaven. I'd have traded my pancakes for sleep, but Pete's response squashed that dream. Besides, I didn't come here for sleep, I came for information.

"Doors open at five o'clock, first come, first serve. Can't be late 'cause them doors get locked when they have enough people to fill the beds."

Could I make it until five?

"Listen here, Scotty boy. You come along and stick with me, and I'll show you the ropes. But get eatin', boy. We gotta hurry," Pete bellowed again.

No one had called me Scotty since I was nine, but I didn't correct him. I'd walked into an opportunity, someone loose-lipped, willing to show me the ropes and let me stick with him. But why the hurry? It felt like hours of daylight stretched before us with nowhere to go.

I didn't rush my pancakes, but instead watched a few people come and go through the metal door. When the clock on the wall showed seven o'clock approaching, Pete's agitated hand formed little circles in front of my face, a motion saying, "Hurry." Determined to take a cup of coffee with me, I picked up our Styrofoam cups and asked, "Black or cream?"

Pete flashed his easy grin. "Black and sweet. I take mine black and sweet."

His chuckle led to a fit of coughing. I hesitated for a moment, not sure if I should do something, but he motioned me away with his hand. I turned in the direction of the man he called D.J., but he flipped his empty cup upside down on the table without glancing up.

After we exited the church's side door, Pete stopped to light up a cigarette from the pack tucked in his shirt pocket. We walked through the midst of the morning rush hour with cars at a stand-still, drivers waiting to get past the red light. Dense pedestrian traffic hurried in all directions. Pete could move for an old man, but I kept up, intrigued to see our destination. He darted to a city bench near a busy intersection. Plopping on the bench, Pete reached his weathered hand into a plastic grocery bag he toted around with him. He produced a large and rugged piece of cardboard with "Homeless and Hungry" scribbled on it in black marker. He stationed the sign in front of him and reached in to retrieve a large plastic cup, the kind you might get with a convenience store soft drink. It had "God Bless You" written in marker across the front.

I stood there for a moment, my jaw slack. Hungry? We had just finished devouring a huge plate of pancakes. And panhandling? I'd never imagined myself begging on a street corner. I'd always taken some pretentious pleasure in being a giver, not a taker. But today, this is what I needed to do.

I took the final gulp of my coffee, shook out the residual liquid, and moved toward the bench, only to meet Pete, extending his hand and blocking my movement.

"No siree, Scotty boy. One to a corner. Nobody'll be feedin' the cup for two of us." He reached into his plastic bag and retrieved another smaller piece of cardboard with "Homeless and Disabled" printed on it in amateur block letters. Pete held it out in my direction. "Now limp a little and get on outta here. Find a corner a block or two away with some different traffic. I'll see you in a couple'a hours. We ought'a have enough to get us a burger and some refreshment for tonight, iff'n you know what I mean." With a gleam in his eye and a suppressed grin, he turned his face away, looking pitiful for the crowd.

My cheeks flushed red, I rotated the sign toward myself and walked to the next block. I didn't have to panhandle. I could eat at the shelter and didn't care about Pete's idea of evening refreshment. But Pete was crucial to my plan. He knew the streets. He'd be a big help to me. I couldn't go back empty-handed in two hours. So I located a busy spot near a crowded corner, void of a bench. I sat on my backpack on the ground and propped up my sign, holding the foam cup upright to receive my beggar alms. I tugged the visor on my cap and kept my eyes lowered in case someone recognized me. People stared at me pitifully, some swung closer to the building to avoid me, and a few pulled out coins or a one-dollar bill. Unsure of the protocol of panhandling, when the first person dropped some coins in my cup, I glanced up and said,

"Thank you kindly." That became my mantra of the morning. Two hours and $27.50 later, Pete sauntered up the sidewalk with a large grin. He reached for his cardboard sign as I stood to join him.

As I followed Pete into the diner, the word *retro* might have described the décor. But I'd been a preppy teen. Retro for me was far from this shadowy diner. Dark-green speckled plastic, patched with tape in numerous spots, cushioned the chrome base counter stools. I followed Pete's lead to a counter seat, but when it wobbled with each movement I made, I convinced him to slide into a booth. Stale cigarette smoke clung to the curtains and mingled with the heavy odor of grease drifting from behind the counter.

A waitress in jeans and a black polo with *Larry's Diner* embroidered on the pocket, spread two paper placemats in front of us and topped them with silverware wrapped in a napkin. Her nametag said *Kimberly*. "What'll you have?"

Pete's booming voice echoed through the diner. "I'd be right grateful for some of that there coffee." He pointed toward the coffeepot behind the counter. "Then a big old burger and fries."

The pancakes still sat heavily in my stomach, but I ordered a grilled cheese sandwich.

Pete and I sat over a $3.80 lunch for almost two hours. Each time she went past our table, Kimberly refilled our coffee cups and wiped up the coffee spill and stray cigarette ashes from the shaking of Pete's rheumatic hands.

"So Pete, are all of those people who were in St. John's homeless? Or do some just come for the breakfast?"

Pete took a drink from his coffee mug, his hand

shaking as he lifted it to his mouth. "People got all kinda different places they call home, Scotty. Some might have a place of their own but need help gettin' food now and then."

"How about you? You live on these streets or do you have a place somewhere?"

"Me and D.J. mostly stick together."

That didn't answer my question, but Pete followed that with a coughing spell. When he recovered, he lit another cigarette and started in on a story about the old steel mill where he once worked.

When the lunchtime foot traffic began to pick up, Larry's Diner filled to its meager capacity. Pete got up to leave, magnanimously slipping thirty-five cents on the table for the waitress. The haphazard cluster of bills in his hand indicated that his take from panhandling far exceeded mine. An old man must elicit more sympathy than a young man, even with a proclaimed disability.

"I'll catch up with you later, Scotty."

"Hey, Pete. Hold on a minute. Where will you be eating and sleeping later? Do you go to the place on Stanwix?" I couldn't afford to lose this connection. When and where might I hook up with old Pete again?

"Naw. Ain't fer me. Me and D.J. got us a vacant building over on Liberty. A storage shed in a parking lot. Don't think nobody checked that ol' lock out in a year. You come on over if you can't get you a bed at the shelter. Beats being under the bridge." He slipped out the door and disappeared into the pedestrian traffic on the city sidewalk.

Settling back in the booth, I accepted Kimberly's offer of a coffee refill despite the fact that I was already over-caffeinated. With seven hours until the shelter opened its doors, I finished my coffee and set out to find Pete's vacant building. Perhaps I could sneak a few hours of shut-eye. None of my plans for the day would happen without some sleep. Why in the world did I decide to do this?

2

Claire Bassett

Gentle humming tones sounded from the baby monitor. I glanced at the screen. Drew lay on his back, playful fingers on tiny toes as he warbled at the colorful array of trains cascading from the ceiling. His patience wouldn't last long, so my packing time was limited. Instead of going upstairs as usual, I persisted with my task, thankful for Molly and Jan's help as I loaded my entire kitchen into cardboard boxes.

My table groaned with the weight of stoneware plates and cast-iron pans. How had I accumulated so much in ten years? Boxes, filled and taped, were stacked near the doorway while empty ones sat on my granite countertops waiting to be packed.

The crib springs creaked as Drew stood on shaky fourteen-month-old legs. The hushed moment came while he waited for someone to rescue him, leading to the intolerant scream as the monitor exploded with sound. I hurried to seal the box, stretching the packing tape over the seam before perforating it on the dispenser's toothed edge. Grabbing the thick black marker, I wrote *Storage—kitchen*.

Jan pried the marker from my hand. "You go take care of Drew. We can keep packing. Everything in this room goes to storage. Right?"

My sigh was deep. Tight spasms climbed from my jaw to my temples. "Yes, nothing here will go with me to my parents' home. Are you sure?"

"Yes. Go. We're good here." She placed her hands on my shoulders and turned me toward the stairs. "It's what we came for."

My tired legs ached as I trudged up the stairs. What kind of person left neighbors to do their packing? I peeked around the corner. Drew was on his feet, shaking the sides of the crib, his face red from the outburst. When he saw me, he reached forward with his chubby arms.

Sitting in the nursery rocker, I stroked gentle, circular patterns on his back until the stiffness relaxed into a softness. My shoulders softened as I inhaled the sweet smell of baby and marveled again at his soft, velvet hair. A gentle melody jingled from the mobile, orchestrated by the lazy movement of the ceiling fan. How many mornings had I sat like this? But next week, this room would belong to another boy. One too old to be rocked and stroked. The crib would become a bed, the baby toys would turn into video games, and the gentle tones of the mobile would be exchanged for the music of today's teens.

Twenty minutes later, with a fresh diaper and his little jacket, we went to the front porch to watch for the school bus. It would bring Isabella home from the last day in her kindergarten classroom. Molly joined me, carrying a tray with three cups of tea.

"Jan's finishing the last box and all the cabinets will be done."

We sat on the porch sipping our tea, rocking on white Adirondacks, a contrast to the pots of red geraniums hanging in increments between the posts.

The mild weather allowed the blooms to outlast the typical season. Yet their curled leaves and fading blossoms revealed that they, like me, were on their way out.

I wrapped my hands around the warm cup and looked at my neighbors. "Thanks so much. I couldn't have done this without you."

"It's what neighbors do. Friends help friends."

I took a long, slow sip of my tea, looking around at all that remained to be done. "Can one of you use these chairs? No sense in them sitting in storage if they can be used."

Jan glanced at Molly. "Molly, my porch is full. Can you use these?"

"I'll put them in my sunroom, but only to hold them for you. You'll be back, Claire. This is a temporary move."

"I hope so. I really hope so." The pulse in my throat throbbed, and I fought tears.

"You're doing the right thing. You've been trying to do this all on your own. Let your parents help you. You know they want to."

"I know, Jan. But it feels like I'm giving up. Giving up hope that Andrew will return. And look what I've done to Isabella. Three weeks into kindergarten, and I have to move her to another school, another church. As if she hasn't been through enough. My little girl needs some stability in her life."

Jan set her cup on the tray and leaned closer to me, twining her fingers with mine. "You're her stability. You didn't know the house would rent so quickly. None of this is your fault. You can't do any more than you've done. It's a miracle you haven't fallen apart."

I chuckled. "Who says I haven't? I fall apart a little

every day."

Molly set her cup down and leaned forward. "You're strong, girl. You keep hanging in there. Hey, we've finished up the last of the packing, and we'll get out of your way."

Jan stood to join her. "Call us if there is anything else we can do."

I got up and hugged them before they walked back to their homes, one across the street from me, and the other two doors down.

I sat back down and watched for the school bus. It had all been decided six weeks ago. I'd pondered my options a hundred times. I had minimal workforce skills, and the cost of good daycare didn't make it feasible to take a low-level full-time position. It would be unmanageable to remain in this neighborhood with bills mounting, savings depleted, and health insurance canceled. The house couldn't be sold without Andrew's signature, and that was impossible. When Dad suggested I rent the house out and stay with them, at first I resisted. Three years ago, they had down-sized to a community with patio homes and a high population of senior citizens. I couldn't imagine three more people in that space. And Slippery Rock? I had escaped that tiny rural community years ago. I never expected to live there again. But in the end, I could see no other logical option.

Tension locked in my neck and shoulders. So many changes loomed in the next three days. The renters would relocate from Charlotte and planned to stay in my home for at least six months while they searched for a home of their own. My children would squeeze together in a room the size of my walk-in closet. I was forced to leave my home, friends, and church, and I remained powerless to stop it.

How did one prepare to become a single mother? Divorce would have left some assets and child support. Death would have generated life insurance. But when your husband goes missing, you're left with nothing but a bucket of bills and a house that's no longer a home. If I could have foreseen my situation, I'd have never quit college without finishing. But when I dropped out to get married at twenty-one years old, Andrew was all that mattered.

The brakes on the school bus shrieked, pulling me back from my pointless thoughts to face today's reality. No good ever came from "what ifs."

Isabella bounced down the two steps from the bus at the same time that I reached the end of our walk. I always met her so she wouldn't dart off into the street. Kids did unpredictable things, and Isabella had a mind of her own.

~*~

A bright orange sunrise greeted me when I opened the slats on my bedroom blinds. The weatherman had predicted a sunny day. That didn't seem right. Today should be gray and gloomy, a sorrowful day, a day for regrets. Sitting cross-legged on my bed, I completed my mental checklist. I had packed all of the clothes except Andrew's. They wouldn't go to Slippery Rock but would be boxed for storage. Dad said I should donate them to charity, but I couldn't do it.

When I could delay no longer, I opened the closet I'd been so careful to avoid. I began with his suits, placing them in protective garment bags so they would be ready when he returned. I had no difficulty placing them into the box. Yet as I removed a handful of T-shirts and golf shirts from their hangers, hot tears clouded my eyes. This is where Andrew lived—not the office attire, but the everyday casual work-around-the-house clothes. Even through my blurred eyes I could see him in each one. I held them to my cheek, and the soft cotton absorbed the salty stream.

A glance toward the window told me the orange sunrise had turned golden. I didn't get my gloomy day. Was it too much to ask, God, that He mourn with me?

The rental truck pulled up to the house, followed by my parents' car. Picking Drew up, we jaunted down the stairs to meet them. My brothers leapt out of the truck and dashed toward the children. Bradley scooped up Isabella and spun her as she squealed in delight. Kevin hopped the gate to the porch and began to tickle Drew, his giggle so loud and genuine, it even made me smile.

"I have coffee and doughnuts ready on the deck once the truck is loaded."

"So, no work, no coffee? Is that it?" Kevin teased. Five years my junior, Kevin was in his last year of college. Bradley, the oldest, was already loading the truck with boxes stacked by the door. Isabella attempted to help him by carrying items from her toy box, one by one. As she approached the driveway, I sprinted and caught her arm.

"Isabella, no driveway! You know that."

"But Uncle Brad said I could help."

"No driveway!" I used my sharpest tone and pulled her back onto the porch, but not before I caught Bradley's sympathetic look in her direction. He knew better than to intervene.

It didn't take long to load the truck. It only contained the personal items that would travel about forty-five miles north on I-79 to Slippery Rock. Most of my things would be going into storage. Professional movers would come tomorrow to take the furniture and boxes to the storage facility, courtesy of my father.

We finished and went around back to the deck. Isabella, her hair a mop of thick, spiraled curls, had telltale signs of her jelly doughnut on her chin. "Nana, I'm coming to your house today, and Mommy is staying here."

My mother took a napkin to the messy chin and ruffled her hair. "Yes, sweet Bella. You'll come to my house. We'll have a little extra time before your mama comes up tomorrow. Won't that be fun?"

With hands on her hips, Isabella showed her spunky side. "Well, it will be fun if we can bake cookies."

With a sharp intake of breath, Mother seemed amazed, as though the idea had not occurred to her. "Great idea! We can bake cookies and have them ready for when your mama comes. Won't that be a nice surprise?"

"Nana! It isn't a surprise 'cause she heard us."

Mother smoothed a stray curl from her eyes. "Well then, we'll have to think up another surprise."

With the car loaded, Drew in his car seat, Isabella in her booster and both surrounded by a large array of toys, everyone waved as they pulled out of the driveway. The car curved around the corner out of our subdivision, and I turned to go back inside with my brothers.

But I stopped first, gazing at my home. It had been

a bright, sunny day like this when we moved the furniture in. There had been no brilliant red geraniums potted on my porch, no remnants of the marigolds and impatiens I sowed into the earth last spring. I could see the corner of the swings in the back that Andrew had set up for Isabella. It was just a house when we purchased it. We'd made it a home.

Andrew and I once stood hand-in-hand in this exact spot, gazing at the fine brick home, its handsome rooflines, the brilliant chandelier visible through the window in the two-story entry. A finer home than I'd ever dreamed of. My accountant husband had viewed it as an investment. He'd always been a saver. Unfortunately, the balance of that savings didn't survive his eleven-month absence.

I had fallen in love with Andrew in college—at Pitt where we were both accounting majors. I learned two things at Pitt: I hated accounting and I loved Andrew Bassett. He finished with honors, but I quit to marry him.

Andrew was the accountant prototype—logical, practical, dependable. He was all I ever wanted—the husband I dreamed of. He could give me a home and a family I could nurture.

What was the old saying? *Man plans and God laughs*. Where was my logical, practical, dependable husband now?

Someone touched my shoulder, giving it a soft squeeze, pulling me back from my pointless thoughts. I hadn't seen Bradley step up beside me.

"You OK?"

I positioned a smile on my face. "Sure."

I reached into my pocket and retrieved the envelope I'd prepared. It had *truck rental* written on the front and a check inside. As I handed it to Bradley, he curled his gentle hand over mine, tucking the envelope inside. "I've got this, Sis."

~*~

The kids went with my parents, and my brothers had taken my things away, leaving me alone and vulnerable. I picked up a plate that had somehow escaped packing. How is it that this set of stoneware, glazed in a dusty rose pattern, had once been so important?

The day Andrew and I completed our bridal registry, I saw the set of earthenware dishes. Nothing else would do. Andrew picked up a masculine design of brown stoneware with a tan border. I'd scrunched my face in distaste and he'd laughed. We added the rose pattern to our registry. I found the perfect placemats to match, complete with linen napkins and rose napkin holders. I'd set a flawless table.

I enfolded the loose plate in a remnant of bubble wrap and placed it in a box with mismatched, haphazard pieces, hoping someday to reunite it with the rest of the set. I went upstairs, pulled back the bedspread on one side of my king-sized bed, and sat down. In a few weeks, it would be Isabella's sixth birthday. How would it be possible for me to celebrate? Bella's birthday marked a year since my nightmare began. But for her sake, I'd put on my smile, hand her colorful packages with pink ribbons, and pretend I wasn't falling apart.

With experienced movements, I reached into the nightstand drawer and pulled out the wedding picture

I couldn't bear to be without. As I did every night, I touched a gentle finger to the cold glass that covered my husband's face and wished him a good night. I said a prayer for his safety and placed it on the spot where he had once lain beside me. Reaching for the pillow where his scent had long since been laundered away, I held him close to my heart. I couldn't hate him. Even after all this time. I thought of all of the things he missed—Drew's first steps, Isabella's first day of school, Maxwell's death when he'd curled up in his dog bed and died of a broken heart. If not for the children, I might have done the same.

I slid from the bed to kneel beside it, holding fast to his pillow, feeling tiny and insignificant.

"My God, my God, why have You forsaken me?" Tears threatened, but I held them at bay. "Forgive me, Lord. I know You're my strength in weakness, but right now, I can't feel Your strength. Help me to understand how You're working in my life. I can't see it, Lord."

I gave in to the tears that would saturate this pillow case for the last time before it joined my other belongings in a storage shed.

3

Scott Harrington

Pittsburgh, once a main trading post for those en route to the West, had developed into a striking city. Despite my fatigue, I enjoyed walking through the park at the point of three rivers, where the Monongahela and the Allegheny met to form the Ohio. My eyes drank in the majestic fountain, complimented by a backdrop of impressive skyscrapers with the US Steel Tower standing tall over all the others.

As I made my way toward Liberty Avenue to find Pete's vacant shed, it struck me that, as impressive as the city appeared from a distance, walkers saw all the flaws. Trash littered the sidewalks despite the abundance of receptacles. Grime from the port authority buses blackened many surfaces, and a pungent smell of exhaust permeated the air.

When I saw three parking lots in close proximity, I quickly ruled out the indoor lot. It would have no outbuilding for Pete to occupy. Another lot offered spaces for the adjacent office building, with a gated entrance. Pete's had to be the open-air parking with a small out-building bordering an alley.

A lot attendant stood sentry in a booth at the entrance. I walked by, close enough to see the sign with hours of operation. The lot would close at ten o'clock in the evening. An inefficient lock sagged over the knob. The only access came from inside the parking area, where the attendant watched. I walked around the corner into the alley at the building's backside. My lips pressed together in a frown as a heaviness took over my limbs. No place here to rest my head.

I'd head back toward Stanwix Street at five o'clock and try Three Rivers Mission. Perhaps I'd make another connection. I needed more than just Pete. If I couldn't secure a bed there, I'd come back here after ten to meet up with Pete. I would need to pick up a flashlight with the remains of my $27.50 since the dilapidated shed contained no windows.

Six and a half hours left until the shelter doors opened. I headed in the direction of the bus station, where I could claim a bench. While walking, I began to formulate my plans. Pete should do fine. His constant chatter had given me a start.

At the bus station, I found a bench, stretched my legs out and laced my arms through the straps of my backpack, and dozed. When I woke, I jotted some notes on the pad I kept hidden inside my backpack. I detailed Pete's appearance, his mannerisms, his loud voice, the cough. I wrote specifics about the personal stories he so freely offered. He had worked in a steel mill at one time. I'd need more information about where and when.

I intended to have my name on at least one of the top awards for excellence in journalism after this project. I set my eyes on the Pulitzer. A few local and less prestigious awards hung on my wall, but I hungered to be out there among the best, ready for Charles Harrington to see his son with something besides disappointment.

The project wouldn't be effective unless I lived among people on the street, interacted with them, built relationships. Only then could I collect enough information to develop an outline for my documentary. I would need two more people to provide bios.

Once I left the bus station, a few hours remained before the shelter doors opened at five o'clock. I walked Penn Avenue toward the Three Sisters' bridges. Crossing the Roberto Clemente Bridge to the Northside offered a change of scenery and an impressive view of PNC Park. I found a grassy square that provided a good place to watch people coming and going, where I could enjoy some green space in the middle of a cement world. A street vender sold hot pretzels from a colorful cart. I dug through my backpack and pulled out a dollar.

"I'll have a pretzel, please."

He reached in the canopied stand with a napkin, produced a lukewarm pretzel, and handed it to me.

"Thanks. Are you always in this location?"

He tucked my dollar bill in a leather pouch secured around his waist. "Everyday."

"Does this area get many homeless people? Do they camp out here at night?"

He eyed my frayed jeans. "Not up here. There are what we call Bridge People that have a little homeless community under the railway trestle on East Street. You can find them there at night, but some hang around all day. Guy calling himself Rocko comes by sometimes when I'm closing up and takes the leftover cold pretzels. If you're looking for a place to stay, find Rocko and tell him I sent you."

I tipped my head. "Thanks. I just might do that."

Wrought iron benches had been placed in sporadic fashion throughout the grassy park. I chose one that provided a wide view.

The pretzel's salt awakened my mouth, reminding me I hadn't eaten since lunch. I savored each bite. Large oaks evidenced how long this green expanse had been protected from city expansion. A few green leaves left their branches behind and floated to the grass, beating the autumn deluge that would come in a few weeks.

When the brightness dimmed and the wind picked up, I started my return trip to the downtown area. As I made my way back across the bridge before darkness surrounded it, the September air turned cool, and I walked into the wind. It swept over the open bridge, intensified by moving traffic. Wind stung my ears, along with the whoosh of cars speeding by and an occasional honk from an impatient driver. With my head down, I held tight to the front of my jacket with the broken zipper and turned my collar up.

The visit across town proved to be costly. I had nothing but time on my hands, yet it sneaked past the five o'clock deadline. When I arrived, the shelter was full. I didn't mind since I still needed information for Pete's profile. I'd join him in the little vacant storage shed.

I revisited the diner where we had lunch. The low cost accommodated my skimpy stash. Ten o'clock couldn't come soon enough. After I ate, I hung out around the parking garage like a voyeur, watching the cars coming and going, careful not to stand under the streetlight. No need to call attention to myself. Very few cars remained in the lot, but the gate attendant continued to the end.

Finally, the lights went out in the gatehouse, and the attendant slid into his own car. Turning it toward the exit, his headlights came on and the car disappeared into the line of vehicles exiting the city. I waited about five more minutes just in case he returned for something. Crossing the street, I strode over to the outbuilding like I belonged there and opened the door.

When the door creaked open, whatever rodents had been disturbed scratched and scurried their way to safety. A musty smell of damp wood assaulted my nostrils with its foul odor. I hit the switch on my brand new two-dollar flashlight. Pete and D.J. were already there and sound asleep! How the heck did they get in here? I'd be sure to ask in the morning.

As accommodations went, this turned out to be a miniscule step up from under the bridge. It offered a windbreak from the cold and a semblance of privacy, but comfort proved to be illusive. Pete, on the other hand, slept on what appeared to be an exercise mat. Something he either found or kept here.

Finding a clearing on the wood floor, I pulled out my cardboard and blanket and puffed my backpack for a pillow. D.J.'s eye opened, a decided frown swept across his mouth, and his eye closed again. I lay my aching legs down for what I hoped would be a full night's sleep.

~*~

Exhaustion was the only explanation for falling asleep so quickly. A few hours of deep sleep were followed by a restless slumber until fissures of daylight shone through the ill-fitted door. There was no sign of D.J., and Pete was still out cold. An empty bottle of Black Eagle Bourbon lay beside him. I tried to peer through the slender gap. What time did the lot open? Since no one was in the booth, it would be better to get the heck out of there before I became trapped inside.

Pete didn't budge when I creaked the door open on its rickety hinges or when the blast of cold entered with the hazy morning light. I slipped out and hustled away from the empty lot, heading toward St. John's and a hot cup of coffee.

Well into my pancakes and second cup of coffee, Pete and D.J. walked in.

"Morning, Pete. Morning D.J. I joined you in your vacant shed last night, but you were out cold."

Pete grinned. "That I was, Scotty."

D.J., as usual, had no reply. He knew I'd been there since he had to step around me to leave in the morning.

"So, Pete, how'd you get in there with the parking lot attendant watching? I waited until he left before I sneaked in."

Pete's wide grin caused his bloodshot eyes to dance with light. "It's all in the timin', Scotty. All in the timin'."

Well, that told me nothing.

Taking a long drink of my coffee, I set it down and stabbed a fork into one of my pancakes. "So, Pete, you worked in a steel mill? Which one?"

"Weren't here in Pittsburgh. That was when I was living in Johnstown. Most of the boys headed to the steel mill when we was old enough to get in." Pete's thick Pittsburgh dialect distorted the words, but I'd lived here long enough to work through it.

"You were pretty young? How long did you work in the mill?"

Pete cackled a laugh. "Not too long, Scotty. Them were hot, dirty days. Got me outta there as soon as I could."

Pete didn't need much encouragement. I brought fresh ears to hear his old stories. Boisterous and animated, he didn't answer my direct questions but went off on a rabbit trail-of-a-tale about missing his stop on a boxcar and finding himself in Weirton, West Virginia, having to hitchhike with truckers to make his way back to Pittsburgh.

As I listened, I tried to imagine Pete in another life. Did he have a wife or kids? What else had he done? I peppered a few questions his way, but his responses always included a cackling laugh and vague information.

"Me? I done me a whole load of different jobs in my life. You should'a seen me when I tried my hand at weldin' stuff together. That was a jiagunda fire." He laughed until a coughing fit took over.

I searched his eyes and his exaggerated red cheeks, looking for a younger man. How old might Pete be? Seventy? Maybe not as old as he looked. The bottle could add years to a face.

My attention turned to the left. I tuned out Pete's latest escapade to ponder the man called D.J. He hadn't spoken a word or made eye contact with me or anyone else. He looked younger than Pete. I wanted to say early fifties, but even as I entertained that number, I suspected I had it inflated. Graying hair veined through a light shade of brown. The thinning of his hair created an endless forehead that rested over his deep-set eyes and hollow cheeks. A Ralph Lauren dark green polo, once high quality, now exposed a rip at the shoulder and frays near the hem. He'd been on the streets for quite a while and hadn't weathered it well.

Let's see if the silent man does more than grunt. "So D.J., how about you? What did you do before you hit on hard times?"

If I surprised him by being so forward, he showed no sign. He also lingered before responding, raising his head from its unremitting downward position. Just about the time I had given up hope of getting an answer, he spoke. "I played the numbers."

His eyes turned and challenged me. I let it drop from there. I had a small piece of his story. He'd been a gambler.

Pete gathered up his trash. "Let's get a'movin' fellers."

Yesterday, D.J. had not joined him for panhandling, but this time he stood to leave. Hurrying to keep up with Pete's swift movement, I followed him to the same corner, watching to see what D.J. would do. He claimed his own bus stop bench short of Pete's corner but showed no sign of doing anything but sitting. Before I left Pete to find my own corner, I inquired.

"Does your buddy panhandle? I don't see him getting anything ready?"

"D.J.? Naw. He says he got everything he needs."

I dug a little deeper. "He's a strange one. Eyes a little dark, you know. Kinda scary."

"Naw. Don't you go worryin' none 'bout D.J. He got a lot of stuff to be thinkin' about. Gotta think it outta his self, that's all."

I arched my eyebrow. "What kinda stuff?"

Pete fluttered his hand to motion me away from his space. "Just D.J. stuff. Now get on outta my corner. See you at the diner."

With that, Pete sat down and pulled out his sign. I started to walk away when he called. As I glanced over my shoulder, he tossed me the extra sign. A lady crossed the street, holding the hand of a young child, a girl around five or six. She skipped, her mass of blonde curls bouncing. D.J.'s eyes fixed on the little girl, his expression impossible to define. A prickly cold crept over me. I shook off a shiver and continued to my panhandling spot.

~*~

The endless hours of wandering the streets could make a person go crazy. I planned to be at the shelter on Stanwix in time to get dinner and a bed. I needed to make more connections. In the meantime, with hours to kill, I had a craving for a coffee. Glancing to make sure Pete and D.J. weren't around, I slipped into the coffee shop and took a seat in the far back.

Sipping my caramel macchiato and eating a blueberry scone would've felt routine if only I'd had my laptop. Instead, I took out the old notebook from the bottom of my backpack. As a visual person, I did better seeing things in writing, creating a flowchart, sequencing steps. I would follow three people from their early life to homelessness. What happened? Where did things break down? What distanced them from the other people in their earlier lives? Parents. Siblings. How effective were government programs and non-profits? If I pulled off what I hoped to accomplish, I would pull my audience into each story. Each of the three men would come alive and become real to the readers. A few life changes one way or the other and that might have been them.

Pete would be one of the three. An early evening in the vacant parking lot storage might be helpful. The bourbon should make him loose-lipped. But I needed three bios in the documentary. D.J. obviously had a story, but could I crack that exterior? Also, a gambler wouldn't carry the same level of reader compassion ... and his fixation on the little girl disturbed me. No, I wouldn't choose D.J.

An increase in traffic noise broke into my deep concentration. Horns honked, bus stops filled. It had been two hours. I'd overstayed. Throwing my notebook into the bottom of my backpack, I stopped at the door to make sure Pete and D.J. were nowhere in sight. I still had to protect my cover, and impoverished men didn't choose coffee shops that sold five-dollar espresso drinks

Sprinting back to Stanwix Street, I joined the line creeping toward the door, hoping to gain entrance. Two days in a row I had misjudged my time. Right before the doors closed, shutting me out, I saw a familiar form. The kid in the hoodie from the Tenth Street Bridge. The one with the bulging backpack. He made it through the door before the FULL sign appeared, shutting me out. A destitute teen would be certain to hold human interest. I'd attempt to cross paths with him again.

How does a teenage kid end up in a place like this? Couldn't he go to his parents for help? I exhaled a deep breath as my father came to mind. What would he say if he saw me inching my way up a food line?

My mother would try to hide that information from her socialite friends. My father would try to find someone to sue. I smiled as I imagined them looking at my photo holding the Pulitzer. Would that finally be enough?

~*~

I hadn't planned a trip home until the following week, but when I missed the shelter, I decided to do a short overnight in the comfort of my own bed. There would have been benefits to spending the evening with Pete, but the parking lot outbuilding didn't include the luxury of a shower, and I'd become offensive.

Happy to leave the city behind for a brief reprieve, a slight twinge of guilt reminded me that Pete and D.J. didn't have that option. I claimed a seat at the far back of the bus heading toward Sewickley. We stopped on Church Street, and I exited, making the easy walk to Stella's to pick up a Greek chicken salad to go. A block from my home, Stella's Café offered a touch of panache in the lazy little town with its quaint shops and outside dining.

Bells jingled when I opened the door, announcing the arrival of a customer. Some unknown teen worked the checkout counter. I asked for Stella just as she walked through the swinging door from the kitchen.

"I've been late coming in because I'm taking care of some schmuck's dog while he plays make believe."

I chuckled. She mastered wordplay to the envy of many a writer. With her blond hair bound in a tight knot and covered with netting, she held a tray of desserts for the display case near the door. Effective marketing tool. Everyone coming and going would walk past the cannoli, triple layer chocolate cake, and lemon meringue pie.

I held open the door to the pie keeper, not sure how her slender frame held the tray and balanced it with one hand.

"Admit it, Stel. You love that dog like she's your own baby."

"The dog's great. It's the owner that's two degrees left of normal. I gather you haven't been home to say hello to your shower. You finished in the city?"

"Not by a long shot. Just for the night. I have to go back tomorrow, but I'd love to have a Greek chicken salad and take my favorite girl home with me tonight."

With the tray empty, she rubbed powdered sugar from her hands onto her splattered apron.

"Sorry, buddy. I've got to work."

I humored her. "Well then, I'll settle for second favorite. Can I let myself into your place and take her?"

"*Mi casa es su casa.* You've got the key."

"Thanks, Stel. I'll put her back before I head into the city in the morning. I owe you."

"Yeah, about forty times now you owe me. Think up something big."

With my salad in hand, I turned to walk out the door, pausing when she called after me. "Hey, be careful out there."

4

Claire Bassett

The generic bedroom did nothing to identify the occupant, male or female, young or old. Nothing to hint at hobbies, interests, or even color preferences. The nondescript white walls and tan window blinds posed a stark contrast to the children's bedroom. Their room had served as my mother's guest room, decorated for the cover of a home interior magazine before we converted it to a kid's room. Mine had been overflow storage. The only decorative item was a sepia picture of Bradley, Kevin, and me as children.

I squeezed the last of my clothing into a drawer and forced it shut, a knot settling in my stomach. Twin bed, dresser, nightstand, and a tiny closet. From one spot in the room, I could touch each of those items. An open tray table beside my bed held my laptop. It would serve as my make-shift office.

Dad poked his head through the opened doorway. "You have enough room in here, Claire Bear?"

I smiled. His old nickname for me reached beyond my despair. I was the middle child and only girl. When I was young, Dad would come home from his day of teaching, scoop me into his arms, and ask, "How's my little Claire Bear today?" As a teenager, I'd give him my exasperated sigh when he called me that in front of my friends. I never told him that I really loved hearing that nickname.

"Yeah, Dad. I decided it's better for me to take the small room. I'll only be in here to sleep, and the larger room will give Bella space to play." No use mentioning it offered far less space than any of the bedrooms in my Wexford home.

"I could get a bigger bed moved in here if you'd like."

Where? "Not necessary. The twin bed will be fine."

It would be an adjustment, but perhaps a twin bed would be a better fit than my king-sized. I wouldn't have a glaring reminder that half of it remained empty.

The cumbersome burden had been lifted. No more juggling bills and wondering what to do. I welcomed the respite, and yet, it brought a restlessness, a craving for a future beyond the next day. How long do I wait for word from or about Andrew? He had been gone almost a year. When should I give up hope of his return?

Before moving, I went to the police station and made sure they knew how to get in touch with me.

While there, I asked, "Anything new in the investigation?"

"Nothing new on our end." The officer frowned and stared at the clock. I refused to let him hurry me.

"Can I ask what actions you've been taking?"

He crossed his arms over his chest. "Mrs. Bassett, we told you before. We can't put manpower on an adult disappearance without signs of foul play. Your husband left a note and told you he was leaving. No crime has been committed."

He was wrong. There were laws against things like jaywalking and littering. It surely must be a crime for a man to abandon his wife and children with no means of support and no way to contact him. But it became evident I would get no help here.

I reached into my handbag and retrieved the paper I had prepared. "Here's my forwarding address. Please contact me if you have any information."

I reached across the desk and almost stuffed it into his hand. He took one quick glance at the paper and set it in the desk tray amid a thousand others.

When I left the station, I drove past the home of my sister-in-law, Jenny. No longer Bassett, she had taken back her maiden name once she and Matthew separated. The death of their only child brought the demise of their marriage.

Andrew and his brother had been inseparable. Jenny became the sister I never had. Now I didn't even know where Matthew had moved. Shattered. Like a mirror splintering into a thousand tiny shards, each splinter showing treasured glimpses of how we once looked but remaining forever irreparable.

I slowed my car as I approached the two-story colonial that had once been so familiar to me. I couldn't explain why I felt drawn to drive past there. It's not as if I could knock on her door and share a cup of tea. Too much had occurred. Would I be welcomed? I would cry for my lost sister, but the tears I shed for Andrew allowed no others to remain.

~*~

Mom finished her grocery list. "If you're sure you

don't mind doing the shopping, I'm happy to watch the kids while you're gone."

"I don't mind. It'll be a treat to shop without taking a baby along."

Shopping proved to be an outing in Slippery Rock. Accustomed to having a grocery store minutes from my home, this rural community didn't offer such amenities. Yet it was a pleasant reprieve from the crowded house on this Saturday morning. Mom was happy to avoid the grocery task, and I was thankful to have a few minutes to myself.

I drove the winding roads, my sunglasses guarding against the brilliance that flashed like strobe lights scattering through trees. The leaves showed the first signs of changing their color, an occasional leaf turning brown, gold, or maple red. In about two weeks, this same road would explode into the brilliant colors of autumn.

The unhurried trip to the grocery store ended way too soon. With groceries unpacked, Drew asleep, and Isabella helping her grandmother in the kitchen, I stepped out onto the patio. The air was cool but fresh.

"Back from grocery shopping?" My father sat on the glider, gently swaying forward and back.

"Dad. I didn't know you were sitting here." He always liked the cold.

An open book rested face-down on his lap and glasses perched on the end of his nose. His white hair didn't age him. Instead, it presented a dignified look.

"What are you reading?"

He turned it over so I could see the cover. It was an economics textbook. "This, until my old eyes started blurring. Can't wait for cataract surgery."

"Too intellectual for me. I like a good beach read."

"Sit down, Claire Bear."

I took a seat across from him, drew my knees close, and wrapped my sweater tighter around me.

"Honey, it's been almost a year."

My knees unbent and I sat up straighter, all semblance of relaxation gone. I wanted no part of this conversation but found myself trapped here, short of walking back inside with overt rudeness.

"I can count, Dad. Do you think I don't know that?" My brisk tone chilled the air like wind blowing over the patio, but I hoped it would quell the discussion about to occur. "Sorry, but I live with that knowledge every day of my life."

"I'm thinking we should make the most of this time while you're here. Why don't you enroll, and I'll see what I can do about getting your Pitt credits to transfer?"

Slippery Rock, a community of farmland, had nothing of significance but for the Pennsylvania state university that sat smack in the middle of nothing. My father taught economics there before retiring and now he taught as an adjunct.

"I can't, Dad. I can't afford it. I'm no longer a minor, and you're no longer an employee. I missed the time for a free ride."

"Don't worry about that, Claire Bear. I'll pick up the tuition."

I swallowed before taking a deep breath. "I can't let you do that, Dad."

A fine line wavered between appreciating the help of my parents and guarding against the mindset of a teenager living under their direction.

His feet stopped the movement of the glider. "Think about it. You need to plan for your future. How long will you wait?"

How long will I wait? The question I'd asked myself so many times over. I'd struggled with that question, yet the answer came out so clear and honest it surprised even me. "As long as I have breath, Dad. That's how long I'll wait."

I stood, too cold to stay out there.

~*~

On occasion, I drove Isabella to school, sparing her the lengthy bus ride. On this Monday morning, after dropping her off, I made the familiar trip through the university with its green campus and dignified brick buildings, always clean and well-kept.

Driving past the building where Dad's office had been located, memories competed in my mind. While I hadn't been a student here, at times I came to work with my Dad, and I attended a few youth summer camps. I found comfort here. Perhaps I should consider enrolling.

I slowed down to let two girls cross in front of me. They laughed at something I couldn't hear. An oversized sweatshirt with leggings drew my attention to long, slender legs and a ponytail that bobbed back and forth as she strolled across. Her friend's skinny jeans fit like denim leggings. I guessed them to be freshmen—perhaps eighteen years old. They moved to a grassy area where a dozen or so students gathered, played Frisbee, sat cross-legged in the grass, or just hung out and enjoyed the moment.

No. Dad wasn't right. I couldn't be one of them, and I didn't want to be a student. Nor did I want a career. I wanted to be a wife and mother. Enrolling in classes would be like giving up. Yet I needed to do something. As I passed the administrative building with its towering clock that could be seen throughout the campus, the decision grasped me like a rescue craft. A job—not a career—until Andrew returned. Perhaps something part time. I couldn't stop into Human Resources with my jeans and sweatshirt, but I would go home and check employment opportunities on their website.

Driving home, my mind was occupied with starting a job search. I hadn't wanted a job. All I'd ever yearned for was to be a wife and mother. But at least a job would offer a change from my immobile state.

Back at home, I carried my laptop to the tiny kitchen table and opened the website for Slippery Rock University. Navigating my way to Human Resources, I located the job openings, narrowing the search to part time support positions, and began to scroll.

The open floor plan of my parent's home offered one large space, divided into kitchen, eating area, and living room. That didn't allow much privacy.

On my mother's walk to the refrigerator, she peered over my shoulder. "Job openings? Claire, what an excellent idea."

I took a deep breath and held it. I'd have to remember to sit on my bed when working on anything personal. Her statement triggered my Dad to leap from the sofa as if spring-loaded. "You're not enrolling?"

"No, Dad. I'm not enrolling." I said it with authority, leaving no room for discussion. He must have caught that, because he didn't pursue. He tapped his glasses back from the end of his nose and peered at my monitor. Three of us in a two-foot space, all gazed into a tiny black screen.

"Well, if you're determined to get a job, go see Bob Whitten in Human Resources and tell him I sent you."

I sat at the top of a waterslide, descending slowly, knowing I would pick up speed and splash into a river of dependency. I couldn't allow that to happen. I have two children and must maintain some control of my life.

"Thanks, folks, but I've got this. Let me handle it my way."

Dad's face went slack, and he began to speak, but then his expression turned to something akin to admiration.

Whether from my own limited merit or from my dad's reputation, I was hired to work in the school of education as office support on Mondays, Wednesdays, and Fridays. I felt relief and regret at the same time.

When I told my parents, Mother flew into planning mode. "Now, Claire, you must get appropriate clothing. Jeans and T-shirts won't do."

I refrained from rolling my eyes. "I never intended to wear them to work, Mom. I do have some nicer things."

"Maybe so, but I think a shopping trip is in order. Dad can watch the kids while we go to the outlets."

Mother, a sleek, stylish lady, had always been the perfect match for her professor husband. Never a hair out of place, never without lipstick. She had tried, without success, to breed her refinement into me.

It would be such a throw-back to shop at the outlets with my mother. As a teenager, I would load up my arms with all of my treasured selections while my mother feigned reluctance. She would veto most of them, choose one or two things to purchase, and we would both go home happy.

We drove the short distance to the outlets and began looking in ladies' specialty shops, our roles now so reversed. My mother's arms bulged with stylish business casual that she urged me to try on.

"Mother, I'm working three days a week. I don't need all of that."

"Well, you can't repeat the same three outfits week after week. Try them on."

I enjoyed shopping again—twirling for the dressing room mirrors, walking out to model for my mom, accessorizing. It had been a long time since I'd had a carefree afternoon.

"Now, Claire, we must do something about your hair. It's way too 'sixteen' for you."

I'm sliding, sliding.

Three weeks later, seated in my new office—well, cubicle would be more accurate—I sported a heather-gray pencil skirt and a soft yellow sweater with a deep cowl neck. My hair stacked in the back and angled close to my chin, its subtle highlights blended to create a glowing effect without changing my own warm shade of brown. With guilty excitement, I regarded the image staring back at me. Would Andrew even recognize me?

It was the one-year anniversary of his desertion.

5

Scott Harrington

I timed it correctly and made it through the door of the Stanwix Street shelter. After signing in, I followed the men moving toward the left into a large area set with tables and chairs. A food line had already started at the far end, similar to the breakfast at St. John's. I took my time scanning the room before heading over.

I needed to strike up a conversation and was scoping out my options when I saw the kid from under the bridge. He inched his way up the food line, his backpack secured over his shoulders. I joined the line hoping to catch up with him before the seats filled up.

I reached the front and picked up an empty plate. A lady behind the table tossed a slice of ham onto it. The line kept moving as helpers plopped a scoop of mac and cheese, salad, and a roll onto each plate. I picked up a pre-poured cup of coffee from the end of the table.

Recognition lit the kid's eyes as I approached his table. I set my plate down across from him. "Hi. I'm Scott. I think we stayed at the same hotel a few nights ago."

He chuckled. "Yeah. The Bridge Resort. A real one-star facility. I'm Tyler."

I tested my coffee. Strong, black, and slightly warm. "I can't say I slept much under the overpass. This is the first night I've made it through these doors. Tonight I made sure I arrived early enough. How about you? Have you been back under the bridge?"

"No. I stayed here last night. Can't say it's much better."

I raised my eyebrows. "How could it not be better than hard concrete and traffic whizzing overhead?" .

"Wait 'til tonight. You'll see. It's filled with hacking coughs and body odor. I've got to get a job and get out of here." He took a bite of his mac and cheese. "Artificial cheese. Probably powdered. And the ham's almost too salty to eat. I guess I shouldn't complain. It's free." He picked up his water and drank.

I looked at my coffee and wished I'd opted for the water. "It's a hard life. Some of these fellas look like they've been at it a while."

He nodded. "Well, I don't plan to be one of them. I'm trying to get a job."

"Good for you. It's tough without an address."

"I give my e-mail and check it every day at the library. It's a good place to hang out. I can sit there and read if I have time to kill."

We were interrupted when a man spoke to the whole group. We ate while he provided a reminder about restrooms, showers, cots, and the time for breakfast. Anyone who remained sleeping past eight-thirty would be woken. Breakfast would be served until nine, and everyone had to be out by nine-thirty.

When he'd finished speaking, I picked up the conversation. "How old are you? How'd you end up here?"

"I'm eighteen. How'd I end up here? I keep asking

myself that question. I guess it's part of a long story."

I pushed my empty plate away and leaned back. "I like stories."

Tyler crushed his napkin and placed it on his empty plate. "You want the long or the short?"

I glanced at the clock that read six thirty. "Looks like we have nothing but time." This would definitely be one of the three biographies. I couldn't take notes, so I'd have to listen carefully, remembering details until I could commit them to paper.

"I was nine when my dad took off. My mother liked her beer and drank too much of it. When she did, she'd holler and throw things. My dad always tried to get me out of the house. We'd grab our fishing rods and head down to the river. Sometimes he'd take me to a baseball game. We'd climb up the stairs to the cheap seats. He called it peanut heaven. I guess he couldn't handle life with my mother, so he took off."

I interrupted his flow of words. "Do you see him now?"

"Nope. He left me a note that said he'd get a place for us and come back for me. But he didn't come back. I guess he settled somewhere and managed to forget he had a son."

I saw him glance at his backpack on the floor. He reached his foot and pulled it closer.

"My mother managed to go from one man to another. She moved us around so much that I never stayed in a school for more than one year. You can't make friends that way. I was in three different schools during my junior year. Since I didn't have friends to hang out with, I read. I'd bury myself in a book. That's how I coped. I'd hang out in libraries, and you can imagine the teasing that brought. Even my mother thought I was weird."

I nodded. "Something we have in common. I've always been a reader."

"What's going on with you? You're younger than most of these guys."

I squirmed, not liking the shift. "Just a little down on my luck right now. So where's your mother now? Could she help you out of this mess?" Hopefully, the topic would stay right where I needed it to be.

Tyler sat back. "About a year ago, she met Bob. She thought she hit pay dirt, but he's scum. He used to rough me up when she wasn't around. Never hit me in the face or anywhere it would show, but if I said one wrong word when she wasn't there, he'd punch me in the gut or push me up against the wall. Well, she married him, and we had to move again. Who moves their kid in the last quarter of his senior year? He shook his head.

"As soon as I graduated, Bob took a job in Corpus Christi working on an oil rig. They gave me a polite invitation to move to Texas with them, but I declined. I took a job with a landscaper and rented an efficiency room. It was pay-as-you-go. When the seasonal work stopped, I couldn't pay, so they made me go."

"Can you contact your mother? Maybe she could help you financially."

"I wouldn't even if I could. She left and didn't give me an address. Said she'd call, but my phone's been turned off."

"If you know Bob's last name, it shouldn't be too hard to reach them."

"Not a chance. She wouldn't help me. Besides, I'd rather stay here than live off of Bob's money."

Eighteen years old and he had no one. "Have you

ever looked online for your dad? Shouldn't be too hard to locate him. He might be living right in this area."

He raised his eyebrows. "You mean after he abandoned me and left me with a drunkard? No thanks. I'm going to get out of this mess on my own. In fact, I have a chance to make a few bucks right here at the shelter."

"No kidding. They're hiring you?"

"Not exactly hiring. Just odd jobs. I'll be doing deliveries. I've got my first one scheduled tonight."

I glanced at the clock. It was approaching eight. "Tonight? This late? What are you delivering?"

"Don't know. Don't care. It's forty bucks."

"Hey, Tyler. You need to know what you're getting into here. Sounds a little shady."

He reached one hand in his pocket and retrieved a few coins. "I have exactly forty-seven cents. No way am I turning down an easy forty bucks."

I backed off a little. I didn't want Tyler to become defensive. "So who'd you talk to? Did you approach them looking for some work?"

"No, Jim approached me. He was just trying to help me out, probably because I'm the youngest one here. He said that some of these guys are satisfied with their life. They don't care about getting off the streets. But a young guy like me, well he said he'd do what he could to help."

"So how are you doing deliveries without a car?"

"They have one I can use. Jim said they're just short on manpower."

I didn't like the sound of this. Short on manpower that late at night?

He craned his head toward the entrance. "In fact, I see him now. I better get moving. Nice to talk with you."

"Just be careful."

Tyler walked toward a hefty man standing by the entrance, hands on his hips. His T-shirt stretched over a protruding belly, but his biceps looked like he managed to visit the gym. A military haircut did nothing to compliment his full, bristly face.

Tyler met up with him, and they walked out the door. I made my way to that side of the room in time to see them turn the corner toward the side alley. The daylight was fading, but enough remained for me to see through the side window. The slats on the blind were tilted, but not fully closed. Tyler and Jim approached a late model car that had seen better days. Jim opened the trunk and handed Tyler a small box with mailing tape wrapped around it. Tyler took the box, and Jim pulled a folded paper from his pocket. They looked at it together. Jim pointed a finger at him, tapped his watch, and Tyler got into the car.

I turned from the window, certain the package contained drugs. Would the contents of that box end up in the arms of teenagers? Teenagers like Edwin?

I walked back into the room where we ate. Some men lingered, talking. Others made their way up the stairs to where the cots were located. I had no heart for starting another conversation tonight. I turned and headed up the stairs. In the quiet of my cot, I pulled out my tablet and jotted some notes from our conversation.

Little by little, as more men came to bed, the hacking noises began, reminding me of Tyler's words. The cots were placed no more than two feet apart, and the odor of so many men in close quarters replaced any fresh air that had been there. I pulled the blanket up over my mouth and nose to shield myself from the germs. Tyler might be right when he said it wasn't much better than the bridge.

I never heard Tyler return, but when I woke and made a trip to the bathroom, I saw his sleeping form, one arm wrapped tightly around his backpack.

6

Scott Harrington

One final look in the mirror before heading to my appointment. With my face clean-shaven and scrubbed free from the sweaty grime, I looked presentable. My hair remained the only change from my normal routine. It wouldn't do to have a professional cut when returning to the streets, so I combed my shaggy hair back to mask the length and headed into the city for my appointment with Ray Brockman, director of Three Rivers Mission. I hoped the interview would provide some insight into the mission's funding and what they did beyond providing a meal and a bed. Thankfully, the office was not adjacent to Stanwix Street. It wouldn't do to have Pete or Tyler see me cleaned up in a shirt and tie.

I couldn't keep my mind off the kid. Tyler hadn't had a break in his life, and he could be headed down a dangerous path. I'd like to help him but couldn't blow my cover. I suspected there were drugs in those packages, drugs that ended up in the arms of teenage kids. Kids like Edwin.

Tightness gripped my chest when Edwin's name entered my mind. Could I sit back and pretend I didn't know? Yet I wanted to stay focused on my project. It'd been a long time coming, and if I pushed him too much, Tyler might cut me off. A young kid like him could end up being the best of the three bios. I should go to the police with my suspicions, but Tyler might find himself behind bars. I wouldn't do that to him. But how long could I protect him before involving the police? I'd stayed silent too long once before.

Arriving at Ray Brockman's office, I shoved thoughts of Tyler to another corner of my mind, one that, I was certain, would be revisited. Equipped with my digital voice recorder and notebook, I opened the outside door to the office complex and entered the first office on the left, with the placard *Three Rivers Missions*. The room was silent except the click of a keyboard. A receptionist, no doubt the one who had set up the appointment, glanced over her thick-framed reading glasses without a pause in her typing. Stuffy air and the rich smell of leather from the deep brown sofa were my only greeting. Despite the fact that I walked into her empty office, she never offered a *hello*.

With a few short strides, I stood before her desk.

"Hi. Am I in the right place to see Ray Brockman?"

"It'd be the right place if he was here. Can I help you?" Her tone remained indifferent and she only slightly slowed her typing. I made a mental note—rude receptionist, not that it would ever enter my report.

"I'm Scott Harrington. I have an appointment with him at ten o'clock." I glanced at my watch for emphasis, quite certain she already knew about the scheduled meeting.

For the first time, she removed her hands from the keyboard and tipped the glasses up onto her head. "Oh, you must be the newspaper guy."

I corrected her misinformation. "I'm a journalist, but I don't work for a newspaper."

"Same thing. You're the writer. I'm Caroline McMann." She stuck out a red-tipped hand with a ruby ring and a cluster of bangle bracelets.

Ignoring the remark, I took the offered hand. "Pleased to meet you, Carolyn."

"Line," she said adamantly, a slight pout crossing her face. It's Carol-LINE."

I tried to suppress a grin. She had mastered the art of the pout. It actually softened her snarky attitude which, I'm certain, wasn't her intention. I made a career out of reading people. Caroline tossed her strawberry-blond hair back and leaned forward, a motion of power. But her eyes gave her away. Her green eyes drilled me but couldn't maintain contact. She covered it with busyness—looking down to move a paper to another stack, glancing at the monitor or her keyboard, smoothing her sweater. Miss Caroline McMann wanted to present a persona of power but covered a deeper insecurity.

"Well, Carol-line," I emphasized the last syllable, "When will he return? Does he know we're meeting?"

"Oh, you're not meetin' with him. He told me to do the interview. I have all of the material you're lookin' for." The more she spoke, the stronger her accent surfaced.

I tried to lighten the moment, aware that my info would be coming from her.

"So, I take it you're not from around here."

"Savannah, Georgia. Born and raised." That brought a momentary smile.

"Beautiful city. What brought you to Pittsburgh?"

"I'm happy to tell you, but it's your thirty minutes." She pointed a finger at my watch.

I let out a whoosh of air. "Well, then, let's skip that

part. Where are we meeting?"

"Right here. Pull up a chair."

She had no intention of moving from behind her massive mahogany desk. My jaw clenched. I couldn't let my annoyance show. I'd asked for the interview. I took a deep breath, found a hard metal folding chair propped against the wall, and pulled it up. She remained seated in her immense leather swivel chair with substantial side arms. I motioned to my digital voice recorder.

"May I record?" That brought the second smile of the day.

"So, you must like my Georgia accent." She stretched out the vowels into two syllables each. "Let me tell you about Three Rivers Missions."

My questions weren't needed. Caroline offered information, walking me through all aspects of the organization.

The thirty minutes turned into forty-five. Caroline proved herself a worthy source of knowledge, despite her snarky attitude. Halfway through the interview, my list of adjectives had grown. Rude, snarky, sassy, and cute. But I needed to stay focused. I wasn't writing about Caroline McMann.

I turned off the digital voice recorder and stood.

"Thank you for the wealth of information."

"Wait." She reached behind to a file cabinet and retrieved some brochures. "These repeat some of what I've told you, but there's contact information and some great pictures." She flipped through them to identify each one. "Three Rivers Mission. That's the one on Stanwix. South Hills Safe House. This is the one for abused women. Clearway. This is the drug rehab facility in Westmoreland County."

I took the three brochures and flipped to Clearway. "And this is the one that's a profit-making facility? The other two are non-prof?"

"That's right."

"Carol-line," I overemphasize the second syllable of her name. "Thank you for the time and for sharing your knowledge with me."

"You're welcome. Say wonderful things about us in your paper."

This time, I felt compelled to correct her. "I'm a freelance journalist. What I do will result in a documentary, both broadcast journalism and in writing. As a freelance, I'm not sure where this will end up. I don't have it contracted."

"So this could all be for nothin'?" She frowned.

My smile was probably condescending. "Well, my work always gets picked up somewhere. I've won a number of awards."

"Really?" She sounded impressed. "What were they for?" She leaned forward, elbows on her desk.

With the reading glasses in her hand, her bright green hypnotic eyes made me forget about the snarky side. When I found my voice again, I said, "I'll bring copies of a few things I've done so you can read them."

Why did I say that? I had too much to focus on already.

"I'll look forward to that." She motioned to the chair I had vacated, tapping her red nails on her desk. Like a scolded child, I folded the chair and returned it to its spot against the wall.

I opened the door to leave.

"Oh, and Mr. Harrington...?"

"Scott," I corrected her.

The bright green eyes penetrated into mine. "Scott.

What brought me to Pittsburgh? Boyfriend. Followed him here. He dumped me. Too humiliated to go back home. That's the cliff notes' version."

I shook my head. "A very foolish man."

She gave up yet another smile as I pulled the door closed behind me.

~*~

Ginger snored at my feet while I reviewed my notes. I'd adopted her as soon as I finished college. Edwin and I had begged for a dog, but no pets were permitted in the Harrington estate. Mother freaked when Edwin found a stray and stole it away in his bedroom. His marbled black and white fur matted into dried clumps, making his breed obscure. We named him Tramp because of his mangy look. We managed two days of complicity before discovery. Tramp got the boot immediately. Leticia called animal rescue to pick him up. Edwin and I had noses pressed to the bedroom window as the van pulled away with our first and only pet. Leticia then proceeded scrubbing every surface that Tramp had touched, fully erasing him from our lives.

I dreaded putting on my scrubby clothes and heading back to the city, but the empty spaces on my flowchart compelled me to get moving. The absence of a third chart presented a growing concern. I had to find another subject. Two wouldn't make it. D.J.—did I dare try to open that door? He locked himself up about as tense as a man can be. But on the plus side, he always hung around Pete, making him accessible. That in and of itself proved interesting.

The doorbell broke my concentration. I peeked through the blind. Stella.

"Hey, Stel."

When I opened the door, she stood there with her hands on her hips, a small brown shopping bag dangling from her wrist. "Bad news, neighbor. Someone broke in and stole your dog. He's not in my house."

I grinned sheepishly. "Guilty. I only had an hour or two, so I didn't stop by the café."

"A real shame, because the special today was tilapia with mango salsa, which I happen to know you love."

"Ahh, you're killing me. I'm ready to make a frozen pizza."

Stella flinched and covered her mouth in distaste. "You mean, the kind with cardboard crust?"

"Guilty again."

"You're one lucky man, Scott Harrington. I happen to have a take-out special with your name on it." With that, she reached into the bag and retrieved a container. "And don't go feeding cardboard pizza to our dog."

"You're the best! Did you bring something for yourself? Can you stay?" I took the meal and raised my hand for a fist bump.

She touched her knuckles to mine. "Nope. Gotta keep moving. Don't forget to return Ginger. I'm kinda getting used to the old girl."

I closed the door behind her and turned to take my meal to the table when I glanced out the window. Stella didn't walk in the direction of the café. She turned toward her home. I had the uneasy feeling she had given me her lunch.

~*~

Back on Stanwix Street, I sat alone at Three Rivers Mission eating meatloaf, canned green beans, and mashed potatoes made from an instant mix. I was disappointed I hadn't seen the kid anywhere. Having secured a bed for the night, I took time now to scan the room. I made my way around, trying to find a suitable third. Nothing caught my eye, but I managed to strike up a dialogue with an older fellow anyway. A little too much like Pete—same age bracket and signs of alcohol abuse. I needed a little more variety than that.

I meandered over to another man, middle-aged, shabby clothing but clean, close cut hair, and a clean-shaven, coffee-brown face.

"Hey there. How you doing today?"

His eyes darted around the room as though looking for a place to escape. He mumbled an incomprehensible string of unrelated words. His gaze shot back and forth again, and he walked away.

Either mentally ill or stoned. As I turned, a cluster of older men sat at a table. I stopped by and introduced myself. Jack, Charlie, and Luther politely returned the introduction then went back to their conversation, ignoring my presence. I was striking out.

Around eight o'clock, I spotted Tyler coming in the front door with the guy he'd called Jim. He towered over Tyler with his barrel chest thrust out and hands that made sharp movements as he talked. They finished their conversation and strolled into the kitchen where a meal had been saved in the warmer. Jim left and Tyler took his plate to a table. I hung back for a few minutes, not wanting to seem too anxious. I meandered over to the counter where coffee and water were available, poured myself a glass of water, and acted surprised when I saw Tyler sitting there.

"Tyler. How you doing tonight? How'd you get a late meal?"

"Hey. Doing OK. I just got here so I didn't have a chance to eat earlier."

I played dumb. "But the doors lock when it's full. If you're not here by five, you have a slim chance of getting in."

"I told you I'm doing some errands for them." His annoyance was evident.

I nodded slowly. "Oh, I remember. Deliveries, right?"

"Yeah."

"Ever figure out what you're delivering?"

"Told you, I don't know and don't care. Why you so interested? What's it to you?"

Edwin's face crossed my mind, but this wasn't the time or place for that. "Long story, buddy. Long story." I shook off the memory. "But I am concerned about you. I'd hate to see you go from bad to worse."

"I suspect it can't get much worse," Tyler spoke while he took a mouthful of potatoes.

I pursed my lips. "It sure can, Ty. It sure can."

His head shot up, and he wore a strange expression. "My dad used to call me Ty. He's about the only one who ever did."

Our eyes met, and I nodded in understanding. "What do you prefer?"

He started to say one thing but switched gears. "Either is OK."

He returned to the task of eating.

Of my three sleeping experiences, the bridge, the vacant shed, and the shelter with cots in uniformity, I chose the vacant shed. This place offered a hot meal and a shower, but the stench of forty men spaced not much more than two feet apart reeked.

The plastic mattress crackled with every turn of my body. How often did they sanitize these things? Hopefully, every day.

I recapped my discussion with Tyler so I'd keep it fresh in my mind until I could preserve it on paper. Once we put the topic of deliveries aside, we managed to talk all night. His bio would be a perfect story since I had details of several childhood experiences. I should be able to find his father's name with a little cyber surfing. If I could locate and get his dad's side of it, well, that would ice the cake. The kid had potential.

According to him, he did well in school without any help or encouragement. He couldn't graduate with honors since he never remained in one place long enough to meet their requirements, but that made it all the more remarkable that his percentages were so high. He shrugged when he told me it came easy. It would be something if he had a chance to go to college. Could we solicit donations to help offset the cost?

7

Claire Bassett

I walked through the propped-open door to our office complex.

Susie peeked up over her computer and smiled. "Hi, Claire. Love the sweater."

"Thank you. How are you this morning?" What a delicious false sense of normalcy. Three days each week for eight hours I could forget. I would stroll along the brick walkway, greeting folks with casual talk. People didn't know, so there wasn't an unspoken awkwardness hanging over every word.

Until I stepped in my car to return home.

Then it all flooded back to me. That awful day when brakes screamed, sirens shrieked, and tears flooded. Three weeks later came the succinct, gut-wrenching note. Would there ever be a time when I walked through a day without the knowledge that Andrew lived somewhere out there, beyond my reach?

I reached my cubicle in the back corner of the office complex. Not many people stopped by my desk, mostly professors leaving some job for me to do. I reviewed my to-do list for the day and sequenced the tasks—file syllabi, work on supply inventory, and run a bulk mailing to the post office. As I worked, I drank in the smiles from Drew and Isabella captured in the framed photo on the side of my desk.

To avoid unwanted questions, I didn't display a family picture. Instead, I filled the other empty space with a plaque of quirky plant life and a Ralph Waldo Emerson quote: *The earth laughs in flowers.* Andrew and I had purchased it from a souvenir shop on our honeymoon in Key West. He used the word *quirky* for the cubism flowers fashioned in brilliant hues. Then I flashed a quirky grin to match. The plaque served as my remembrance of him. I could peek at it and remember our laughter.

"Morning, Claire. I missed seeing you yesterday."

I turned my head toward the voice. Jonathan Payne took a seat in the chair beside my workspace. We had forged an early bond since both of us were new to the university, although he taught and I served as a part-time, tucked-in-the-back-of-the-room errand girl.

"Hi there. Oh, I don't work on Tuesdays. Remember, I'm three days a week. Monday, Wednesday, and Friday."

"Oh, yeah. Forgot." He pointed toward my cork board. "Hey, I feel honored. You have a picture of me above your desk."

I had printed a website page that showed photos of all faculty in the Department of Education so I could begin to match names and faces when someone came in to see me. "I have a copy with all the faculty above my desk. You're one of many."

He placed his hand over his heart. "You wound me. Does that mean I'm not special?"

I laughed at his antics. "You're all special. What can I do for you today?"

He broke eye contact and fingered the buttons on

the cuff of his sleeve. "I wanted to see if the schedules are ready for the spring semester."

"Uh, I don't have anything to do with schedules. Stephanie does all of that." I placed a question in my tone to indicate he should have known that. Schedules were always a big deal for the whole department.

"Oh, sorry. Temporary brain freeze." He flashed a delightful, boyish smile that melted his features into a charming youthfulness. He hummed or whistled while walking with the fluidity of an athlete, and he had the ability to make me laugh. Levity was so rare these days. I savored those moments, enjoying the taste of it again.

I cut him some slack, although everyone knew who created the schedules. "I'm with you. It's hard being a newbie. Too much to remember."

Glancing at my children's pictures, he settled back in the chair, making no move to see Stephanie.

"Your little girl reminds me of my niece." He began to tell me about the impetuous four-year-old named Hannah. A master storyteller, Jonathan brought laugher throughout the exchange. I found myself joining in and talking about Isabella and Drew. After about fifteen minutes, I stole a glance at the clock and at the paperwork in front of me. I wasn't paid to socialize, even with faculty.

Jonathan must have seen me peek at the clock, because he did likewise, glancing at his watch. "Goodness, it's almost noon. It's beautiful outside. Why don't you grab your lunch and join me down in the courtyard?"

He stood as if it were a settled decision. The pulse in my neck throbbed. I started to decline but hesitated. I had to eat my lunch somewhere, and it would be refreshing to get some sunshine. I took a deep breath, my muscles tensing. *Relax, Claire. It's only lunch with a colleague in a public place. Just someone to talk with while we eat.* "Sure. I'll be right down."

Thankful that Jonathan didn't wait for me, I arched my back, stretching away tension. I reminded myself what this was and wasn't. We were colleagues who happened to be a man and a woman, a fact that shouldn't matter among friends. I slipped my jacket over my arm and opened the desk drawer that held my thermal lunch pack. As I stood, my hand brushed against the colorful flowers blooming on the plaque. *The earth laughs in flowers.* I shut my eyes, took a deep breath, and walked to the elevator.

The cool air and brilliant sunshine created a perfect fall day. A smell of cut grass drifted in the breeze—the scent of fresh and new. Jonathan waited on a bench seat. Scanning the arrangement, I could choose to share the bench or sit across the walkway from him which would prohibit comfortable conversation. *What to do?*

Jonathan solved my problem before I reached him. "Let's go on over to that table." He pointed toward a concrete structure with surrounding benches. "I didn't think you'd see me if I waited there."

I breathed a silent thank you. We sat at the table and each opened our packed lunches.

Andrew and I always gave thanks at mealtime. I closed my eyes and sent up a silent word of thanks.

"So, Claire, what do you enjoy doing when you aren't helping faculty at the Rock?"

What did I enjoy? Had I enjoyed anything in the last year? I had to think back. I measured everything in my life in terms of before and after.

"Well, I enjoy cooking. And I used to do a lot of scrapbooking and paper crafts."

"Paper crafts being?" He tilted his head.

Thoughts of the things I had created brought a smile to my face. "Cards, gift boxes, gift bags, tags, flowers. Once I made a full flower arrangement from tissue and crepe paper. Wait, I think I still have it in my photos."

I retrieved my phone and clicked on the photo app. As I swiped through them, a knot caught in my chest as Andrew smiled at me through a thumb-sized icon. I paused only a moment before scrolling to find my flowers. Clicking it to enlarge, I turned it for Jonathan to see.

"That's paper?" He widened his eyes. "No way!"

Pride crept into my voice. "Yes, sir. Everything except the vase and ribbon."

White daisies with bright yellow centers interspersed with pink carnations and red roses. Green stems with tiny leaves and delicate green fern accented the colorful blooms. A soft green ribbon surrounded the tinted base to provide a finishing touch. The slow process to add such intricate details to each piece proved to be tedious work. Jenny had pleaded with me to make one for her. Three of her flowers were completed. But that was before.

The cloud in my spirit must have crossed my face. "So why the sudden sad look?"

I couldn't talk about it. Wouldn't. "So many of my things are tucked away in storage. I'm going through some temporary changes right now."

Jonathan nodded, and I made an abrupt subject change. "So, what does Jonathan Payne enjoy doing when not teaching wannabe teachers?"

"You've already heard about my precocious niece, Hannah. I love visiting her and spending time with family. Hobbies? I'm an amateur photographer. Love camping, taking scenic pictures, and, when I can, pictures of wildlife."

"Photography? I'd love to see some of your work." *Why did I say that?* The words just blurted out. *I can't encourage a personal relationship here.*

"I'll bring some in to show you. Better yet, I'm headed to Lake Arthur this weekend to do some photos. Why don't you join me, and we'll make it a picnic? You can see how I set up a photo shoot."

A heaviness settled in my chest. "Jonathan, you know I'm married?"

He hesitated before responding. "I heard you're not together."

Tears welled in my eyes. So, I had become the topic of whispered conversation. What else did he know?

"That's also a temporary situation. I can't go to Lake Arthur with you." I spoke with decisiveness, allowing no misconception.

Jonathan nodded and appeared to be measuring his next words. "Are you certain about that? How long have you been apart?"

None of your business. I shifted on my concrete bench. My gaze darted, looking for a reason to escape.

I felt a touch on the back of my hand before he folded his hand under mine, holding it with gentleness. "I'm sorry. I didn't mean to upset you."

It had been so long since a man touched me, other than familial hugs with Dad. My hand burned with the pleasure of resting in his while my heart swelled with guilt. I allowed it to remain for a few sweet moments before I lifted it from his. Then I touched his arm with a gentle pat so he wouldn't think he'd offended me. I couldn't speak. I didn't trust my voice, and I wouldn't have known what to say anyway.

"I'm sorry if I made you uncomfortable." Gentle eyes replaced his usual cheerfulness. "I'd like to spend some time with you and get to know you better. I can't imagine how hard this is for you. But be careful that you're seeing things the way they are and not what you wish they were."

An argument perched on my tongue, but he looked so sweet I couldn't give the words life. I already missed the warmth of his hand.

"And may I keep asking until you're ready?"

I was ready to shake my head, but he lifted his brownie to me like a peace offering. I broke off a tiny corner and ate it while he ate the larger piece. Our shared brownie, my unspoken assent.

~*~

That evening, with the kids tucked in bed and my parents dozing in front of the TV, I climbed into my tiny twin bed. Lying in the claustrophobic room, Andrew and Jonathan competed for my thoughts. I hungered for human touch. I caressed my hand where Jonathan had held it, the warmth of that moment flooding my mind, refusing to leave. A scripture flashed through, interrupting. "Take captive every thought."

I sat upright, reaching toward the nightstand. Lifting the wedding picture from my drawer, I gazed into the happy faces for a few moments before loosening the back latch to retrieve the note. Not sure why, since I had memorized the words.

It had been opened and closed so many times the creases began to come apart, defacing Andrew's scribbled handwriting. The words had not changed. It still didn't say, *I love you, I'll be back, Wait for me.* It still contained the brief cryptic message, *I have to leave. I can't handle this guilt.*

Anger boiled to the surface. My hand clenched into a fist as it held the slip of paper. "Well, guess what, Andrew. I can't handle the loneliness. I can't handle not knowing if you're dead or alive. Did you think about that when you walked out? If these were your last words to me, couldn't you at least have said you loved me?"

I crushed the note into a ball and pitched it across the room.

8

Scott Harrington

I sat on a bench a block away from Three Rivers Mission. For the past week, I'd spent most of my nights there talking with Tyler and now had more than enough information to write his bio.

During the daylight hours, I hung out with Pete. Although he talked freely, I had to dig for anything personal. Pete held that close to his vest. I'd have to spend a few nights at the parking lot shed hoping the bourbon would make him loose-lipped. I needed to figure out how to get by the gate attendant. Otherwise, Pete would be passed out.

But today, I had another undertaking. Tyler left the shelter every night to make a delivery. Sooner or later, he'd get caught. Even if he didn't, I could no longer sit back and pretend I didn't know what was happening.

I watched for Tyler. Maybe I'd see him outside of the shelter. It was impossible to talk about it within those walls.

I caught sight of him walking toward me, edging around slow-moving pedestrians. He either didn't see me or hoped I hadn't seen him. He'd been defensive the last time we talked.

"Hey, Tyler." I stood up and called to him as he

neared the bench. "I've been looking for you. Where've you been all day?"

He turned his head my way, but his gaze fleetingly circled the area. "Told you, I hang out in the library." With jerky movements, he turned his body so he faced away from the shelter. "I was just headed to Stanwix Street for dinner."

He had a facial tic. I hadn't seen that before. "I have a better idea. I can't handle that food tonight. I managed to get a little cash panhandling. Let's go get a big, juicy burger. My treat."

He scanned the area again. "I don't know. I need to see Jim by seven thirty."

"Plenty of time. Didn't you say he'll save you a bed?"

"Yeah, but not for you."

I waved my hand dismissively. "I told you. I can bunk with my old friend, Pete. Hamburger, French fries, ice cold Coke?" The words hung between us, temptingly.

He bit his bottom lip, rubbing his hand over his neck. "I guess."

He took a few tentative steps away from the shelter, and I fell into step beside him.

We walked two blocks and entered Larry's Diner. Within minutes, we were sipping on soft drinks and waiting for our order.

"How you been, Ty? You look a little stressed today."

He took a long drink through the straw in his Coke. "No, I'm fine."

"You upset with me about something? You seemed a little abrupt yesterday." Maybe he would talk about his night deliveries without getting defensive.

"I'm just trying to get off these streets. I save every penny I earn and put applications in everywhere I can. But nothing happens. No family. No friends. I'm just tired of being alone."

Tyler's wheat-colored hair and spattering of freckles gave him a youthful appearance, even less than his eighteen years. "You have one friend. I've enjoyed getting to know you this week."

"Yeah, well, I need to be careful about..." His words trailed off and he cleared his throat.

"About what?"

"Nothing." He sat back, putting distance between us.

"About making friends in the shelter? Does Jim have a problem with that?"

Tyler rested his head against the back of the booth, his shoulders sagging. "He doesn't like talkative drivers. They can get hurt."

My chest tightened. "He told you that? He threatened you?" I clenched my fists. "Let's get you out of there. Come with me tonight and meet Pete."

The conversation halted when the waitress arrived with our burgers. Tyler eyed the plate hungrily, raising it to his nose and breathing in the grilled aroma. He picked up the ketchup and squirted a stream of red onto his fries.

"So what about my question? Will you come meet Pete? We'll get you away from that business."

"You don't get it. This city's not big enough. The only way I'll get out is to leave Pittsburgh. I have nothing holding me here. Maybe I'll have better luck getting a job somewhere else."

"Every delivery you make puts you at risk. Any

one of them could end up in a bust. And every delivery puts more drugs on the street. Can you live with that?"

Tyler jutted out his chin and glared at me. "You're always judging me. I didn't choose this. Once I realized what was happening, I was in too deep. I'm trying to get out. And don't blame me for drugs on the street. They'll be delivered with or without me."

We finished our burgers in silence, and Tyler's temper appeared to cool. I paid our bill, and we stepped out to the sidewalk.

"Thanks for dinner. Two more deliveries. I figure then I'll have enough money for bus fare out of here."

"Unless one of those two gets busted. Change your mind and come with me tonight."

"Can't." He began to walk away.

"I can help you." I called to his departing back.

Tyler turned his head, surprised. "You?" He eyed my frayed jeans and broken zipper. "How old are you, Scott?"

"Thirty-three. Why?"

"Well, I'm eighteen, and I don't aim to be in this situation when I'm thirty-three." He turned and merged with the crowd, heading toward Stanwix Street.

Once Tyler had disappeared from my sight, I walked toward Point Park. I had to get Tyler away from Three Rivers Missions at any expense, even if it meant blowing my cover. I couldn't let him ruin his life while I pretended I didn't know. Once was enough.

With that decision made, another question boiled inside my conscience. How would I expose this drug ring? How ironic that they used Three Rivers Missions to recruit when one of the three branches operated a drug rehabilitation center. Jim kept himself visible at the shelter. How could the director not know? Yet, an organization with a focus on rehab wouldn't...but was the focus on rehab? Or could it be on profit? Were they feeding their own profit-making entity?

A sick feeling settled in my stomach. I would go to the police, but not before I got Tyler out of that mix. Not tonight, though. That might put him at risk. In the morning.

9

Scott Harrington

Hours remained before I'd see Pete and D.J. at the vacant shed. I had to find out how to get in that blasted place before 10:00 PM. and get Pete talking before he passed out. I headed over to the parking garage and loitered until they came.

The October air battered my lightweight jacket. How did the men under the bridge withstand the assault of winter? How would Pete and D.J. deal with it in the drafty shed? Even so, the writer in me began to formulate words to describe the adversities. How could I capture this reality for viewers? Could I transport them from their comfortable easy chairs to the hopeless hardships of these streets?

Standing across the street from the parking lot felt like a stake out. Technically, it was. A few spots offered a good view of the shed so I could move around while watching for Pete.

Darkness descended on the city, making the streetlights and headlights my only means of seeing Pete. After an hour, my chest tightened and constricted with the cold. Fighting off chills, I wanted to retrieve my blanket from the backpack, but that would only call attention to my loitering.

Finally, Pete's boisterous tones reached my end of the sidewalk.

"We need to be a'gettin' you one of them mats a'fore winter is full upon us." I couldn't hear D.J.'s quieter response. Coughing spasms stopped Pete's steps. They were in my sights now, but too far for me to call to them. When the coughing settled, they continued walking and went right up to the parking lot, entered and gave a wave to the attendant, and strolled over. D.J. gave a lift and tug motion to the lock, and the door opened. They had an inside accomplice.

What would I do? I'd waited here for over an hour and I wouldn't be denied. Dodging traffic, I crossed the street and walked into the parking garage. The attendant paid me no mind. I kept one eye on him as I walked over to the shed. He never turned my way, so I opened the door and slipped on inside—that easy.

D.J. stopped speaking. Both of them circled their heads in my direction.

"Hey, mind if I join you tonight? I didn't make the cut for a room." D.J. clicked his flashlight on, illuminating the clutter. I stepped around a few boxes that hadn't been there before.

"Well, howdie do there, Scotty. Close that old door and come on in. We need to be a'keeping that cold out there." Pete's wide grin said he didn't mind at all. D.J.'s glare indicated the opposite. "

Pete held his brown bottle in one hand and a lit cigarette in the other, the tip glowing bright red. It wouldn't take much for this old, dehydrated wood to end up in flames. Mental note: don't fall asleep before old Pete.

Shoving a box to the side, I claimed my spot. "So, what have you been up to in the last two days? Ain't seen you around."

"A little o' this and a little o' that." Laughter came easy to Pete. He managed to find happiness despite his circumstances. "Just about the same ol' thing."

I had a well-fabricated story in mind, hoping to use it as a springboard for discussion. Eager to satisfy D.J.'s suspicions, I told them I worked for a construction crew and the company went bankrupt. Found myself without a job and couldn't pay my rent. Never saw my old man and wouldn't ask him for a dime, not that he would have one anyway. I told my story. Now I wanted Pete's. But before I could turn that tide, D.J. broke his silence.

"What company?" An accusation hovered in the form of a question.

I hadn't considered all the details of my fabricated story and fumbled with an answer, landing on a fictitious name. "Belvedere's," I said, borrowing my mother's maiden name. Her family was in construction but not the building kind. They constructed fine jewelry featuring the purest diamonds from South Africa. But they operated in New York and didn't have exclusive rights to that last name.

"Never heard of it. Where were they located?" He was pushing me, and I needed to close this topic.

"They did most of their work in Beaver County. So, Pete, you said you've done some odd jobs and some welding. Did you go to school for that or did someone train you?"

Laughter in his eyes, Pete shook his head and lifted the bottle for a long drink. He pointed a gnarled finger in my direction. "You's forgettin' I almost burned down the building. No one was a'teachin' me welding."

"Did you go to any school for job training?"

D.J. remained without expression. That was preferable to the evil-eyed glare.

Pete grinned and took another swallow. He held the bottle out, offering me a swig. I put my hand up in a "no, thanks" motion. "Just my old Uncle Sam. They's the only ones gived me any trainin'."

"You mean military? Did you serve?" He had my full attention.

"Yessiree, Scotty boy. We all done served back in them days. You young'uns missed out on a whole lot when they cut that draft and stopped making you work for Uncle Sam. Lots o' buddies and lots o' learning. Them buddies were like brothers."

Good details for the bio. We were seeing widespread respect for our men in uniform. "What branch, and what training did you receive?"

"I served my country in the U-nited States Air Force. Fought in Nam. Got me a medal for outstanding service in a war zone."

"Well, Pete, I'm honored to know you. That's quite a legacy. What kind of job did you do?"

Pete stared at the bottle, took a long drink, stared again like seeing it for the first time. He lifted it and drank again, then settled in to tell his tale, but D.J.'s glare had returned full force.

"I was what they called a Wild Weasel. We had some technical stuff on them planes. We would fly on into enemy air space in North Vietnam and find us them surface to air missiles, called 'em SAMs. We wore these big old headsets that told us when we found us something. It would hiss in our ear. When we did, we'd get a'moving to fire on 'em. Trouble was, we got fired on right back."

I was sitting upright now, arms on my bent knees, taking in every word. "Wow. That sounds like a dangerous job. You came out unscathed?"

"Un-what?"

"Not hurt. You didn't get hurt?"

"Yeah. I got me some hurt." His eyes unfocused, he stared at nothing but a spot on the wall. "Plane got hit, but we glided on down and got her landed. Ended up with some broken bones in one of them POW camps for two years."

Silence filled the space until D.J. spoke. "He doesn't like talking about that. Why don't you leave him be?"

"Sorry, Pete. But, boy, I'm proud to know you. You're a hero. You paid a high price for our freedom."

Our little shed filled with tension, and I would have let this topic fizzle out, but Pete continued, still staring at nothing.

"Folks didn't see it like that when we come back. They booed and spit and called us baby killers. We weren't no heroes to them."

I stretched forward to touch his shoulder. "Well, you are to me, Pete."

Enough for one night. Sooner or later, I'd have to tie this together. No doubt it led to his drinking, which led to his current situation.

Pete curled up on his mat, the bottle cradled close against him, and I glanced at the cigarette butt to make sure he had it fully extinguished. It must have been around 9:30. Not quite ready to sleep, I went through the motions of retrieving my cardboard mattress and my thin blanket from my backpack.

D.J. sat propped against a box, his disapproval stabbing like a knife. I closed my eyes against it but didn't have adequate defense. I'd opened a deep wound and Pete would have to begin healing again. And yet, I now had something good to build my writing on.

Along with my new facts about Pete, I learned two things about D.J. First, he cared about Pete, negating the image of the hard-hearted evil thug I once took him for. Second, on the rare occasion when he spoke, he articulated well. He was a puzzle. But how to get him on my side? That would take some work.

Although wide awake, I closed my eyes and played Dead Fish, our old camping game. When Edwin and I were nine and ten, we started camping in the backyard, the only place allowed since no adults joined us. We were never a camping family, but Leticia fostered our make-believe by packing a basket of snacks and a cooler of drinks. She somehow managed to package marshmallows hot from the oven for s'mores. They lacked the charred crispness but were soft and gooey.

We'd play Dead Fish—who could last the longest without moving, blinking, coughing, laughing. Sometimes I'd open my eyes to steal a peek, certain Edwin did as well. One of us would laugh and bring an end to the game.

Let D.J. think I slept while I processed new data and made some plans and forced my mind to stay focused. It kept returning to the office of Three Rivers Missions. What else could I learn about the rehab center? I told Caroline I'd stop by to show her some of my previous work. I'd been intentional about not rushing back there too soon. But it had been long enough. Tomorrow might be the day, if I could get everything taken care of with Tyler.

The room filled with the soft snoring of sleep. I stole a glance at my roommates. Pete had relinquished the bottle and it sat empty beside him. Even in the dim light, his ashen complexion glowed. That, along with the insistent cough, worried me.

D.J. aimed a flashlight at a book. I strained to see the title but couldn't read it without being too obvious.

I dozed, shallow and restless. Deep sleep eluded me, but I had no desire to leave this building in the middle of the night. I sat up to change positions, my muscles screaming to be stretched. Moonlight or streetlights, hard to tell which, sent a shaft of light along the ill-fitted door.

The spine of D.J.'s book faced me. I chanced moving closer, curious to see what he read. My eyes adjusted and the words on the black and worn book came into focus. Interesting. D.J. was reading a frayed and dog-eared Bible. *OK, Harrington. Rethink the third bio. The silent man may have an interesting story to tell.*

10

Claire Bassett

True to his word, Jonathan asked me out with great persistence. It had become expected and comical.

"Morning, Claire. How about joining me for dinner this weekend?"

"I can't Jonathan. I'm married, Remember?"

He snapped his fingers like he had just recalled that. "Oh, right. Well, how about lunch?" As if that made it different.

"Sorry. Still married."

"Well, I guess I'll have to settle for coffee." He said this as he poured a cup from the office coffeepot and sat beside my desk.

How would he react if one of these days I said yes?

I made the mistake of telling my mother about him.

"Claire, there is absolutely no shame in accepting that invitation. You need to think about yourself and these children. It's been over a year. Honey, I know this is hard, but you have to accept that Andrew is gone. Go out with this man and flirt a little." She tilted her head and batted her eyelashes.

"Mother! I'm not going to flirt. Even as a teenager I didn't flirt."

"Well then, don't flirt. But go to dinner with the man. Put him out of his misery."

In the deepest place, I recognized the reality of her words. My mother had accepted what I could not. Andrew, my husband, my love, was gone, leaving me helpless to do anything about it. Someday I would move on simply because I had no choice. And there might not be a Jonathan waiting in the wings, not one as sweet as he.

The bright sunshine and mild temperatures, a rarity for a western Pennsylvania October, could turn in a heartbeat and bring winter's forerunner in the form of a blustery day. I grasped the opportunity to be in the fresh air while I still could and took my lunch to an outdoor table near my office. Reading on my Kindle while I ate my sandwich, someone startled me from behind. An unexpected whisper spoke close to my ear. "What'cha reading?"

My hand flew to my heart. "Jonathan, you startled me."

He slipped into the chair beside mine.

"Well, that's one way to get your attention. And I guess this is one way to share a meal together." He held up his brown paper bag.

"You are a determined man."

He wiggled his eyebrows and said, "You ain't seen nothin' yet."

"Did you fail syntax when you pursued that PhD?"

He kept in character. "I don't know nothin' 'bout syntax, but I know lots about sin and tax."

The eyebrows wiggled again.

He had me laughing now at his silliness. "Why, you are a naughty man."

"Like I said, you ain't seen nothin' yet."

We resumed eating and changed the conversation to work. New courses would be offered in the spring, and he told me what he would like to teach. Jonathan never took his eyes off of me. They were amazing eyes, drawing me in. I saw kindness and gentleness. The next time he asked, I would say yes. But only to eat. And no promises beyond that.

I didn't have to wait long. While packing up the remains of my lunch, he reached his hand out to take my litter from me. As I held it out toward him, our hands brushed. He bagged my trash and reached again, taking my hand in his. With slumped shoulders and a long exhale, he asked again. "Dinner, Claire?"

I knew he expected a refusal. My hand felt so good resting in his, the mingling of soft and strength. I had become so comfortable with him I had to resist the urge to touch his face with my free hand.

I swallowed the lump in my throat. "Saturday?" My question traveled in the slightest whisper. I heard a gasp and knew I'd surprised him.

"Is that a yes?"

I nodded, the start of a grin forming.

He squeezed my hand. "Yes, Saturday."

I removed my hand and grinned at his childlike pleasure. "I'm late. I need to go back to work."

I left him sitting there as I walked to the door. Before entering, I glanced back to see Jonathan beaming, still seated at the table.

~*~

Back home, locked in my bedroom, I wondered

what in the world I had done. I didn't regret my decision, but I hadn't had a date for more years than I could count. I'd been so caught up in the charm of that moment that I didn't set parameters. This was just dinner—no expectation of a continuing relationship. At some point, I had to make sure he understood.

I didn't tell my mother about my date. I would tell her before Saturday, but I couldn't have her fussing and telling me what to wear. I told Jonathan I'd meet him rather than having him pick me up. I couldn't bring him in to meet my parents like they always required during my teens. That would be too much.

I reached in my nightstand for a pad of paper to begin a grocery list. When I did, my hand landed on the framed picture. I glanced down and had a momentary attack of conscience. I sighed, but I didn't slide it out and talk with him as I did most nights. Instead, I found my notepad and pushed the drawer shut.

~*~

Thursdays were my day off. On this one, I drove into the city.

Buckled into his car seat, Drew fell asleep the minute we started moving. In a rare carefree mood, I found myself singing along with the car radio, while driving to my old neighborhood to have lunch with friends. I would drive by my home and drink in the sight. It still belonged to me, and I intended to return there some day. I didn't know how or when, but that had to be part of my plan.

I turned my car into the subdivision with its

familiar red brick signs at the entrance bordered by crimson barberry shrubs trimmed into perfectly rounded spheres. I gazed at the homes I had become so accustomed to passing. Doors adorned with fall wreaths, mums bloomed in vivid orange, gold, and russet.

Rebecca, Jan, and Molly were all there when I arrived. A secure play area had been cordoned off in the family room for Drew and three other little ones. We started with hugs all around and rapid-fire greetings about how the kids had grown and what was new.

"We haven't gotten to know the new neighbors. The kids are in school all day and both parents work, so we don't see them. I know they're house hunting. I've seen a realtor's car there a few times."

My tongue burned with the desire to tell them about Saturday, tell them about Jonathan, his humor and the attention he showed me. I wanted them to know I looked forward to something rather than always feeling their pity and concern. I would have loved to pull up the school's website and show them how attractive he was. But it was a guilty excitement, so I held my words in check.

When we began to clean up after lunch, Molly pulled me aside. "No word about Andrew?"

I had already provided a cursory update. Why was she bringing it up again? "No. nothing."

I didn't want to revisit this.

"Claire, this is probably nothing, but Jason saw someone who looked a lot like Andrew sitting on a city bench downtown, but he couldn't be sure."

I squinted with narrowing eyes. "Jason knows Andrew too well. How could he not be sure?"

"Well, he was a little distance away, and...and the man he saw looked a lot thinner and, well, not as well groomed." She held something back.

"What are you saying, Molly?"

"The man he saw appeared scrubby and carried a backpack with him." She flapped her hand forward, a gesture to dismiss it as nonsense. "I'm sure it wasn't him, just some resemblance. We better go help with cleanup."

I didn't play the radio on my ride back up north. No song or excitement joined me for the return trip. With a knot in my stomach, my mind filtered this new information. Homeless? That's what Molly didn't say. It couldn't be possible. I had visualized him with a new identify. I had considered a new woman. I had even imagined him dead. But I never thought of him living among the homeless. It had to be wrong. Jason would have known Andrew.

I pulled my car into the driveway, surprised by how fast the trip had gone. My mind had been so distracted it left me with no recollection of the ride. I met Isabella's bus before going inside.

Mom sat at the table, doing a jigsaw puzzle. "Did you enjoy your visit? Did you see everyone you wanted to see?"

"Yeah, it was nice to catch up a little." No part of me wanted to chat with anyone right now. Please, a little solitude.

"Mom, I have a headache and I'm exhausted. I'm going to put Drew down for a nap and take one myself if Bella can stay with you."

"You go rest, dear. Oh, and take some Tylenol first. That should help." She tapped the chair beside her. "Come on up, sweet Bella. Help me find some puzzle pieces."

Drew had played hard and must have been exhausted. He fell right to sleep. I climbed into my own bed, a rarity for me during the daylight hours, Molly's news central in my brain.

Molly and Jason lived across the street from us for six years. We had our first child one year apart. So many evenings we shared each other's porch to catch up on life. Molly and I went to Pilates together. Jason and Andrew hit the golf course a few times each year. Jason could not have seen Andrew without recognizing him. That had to be an error. How well I understood the desire to see Andrew's face in everyone I passed. But it just wasn't so.

Andrew loved Jason. He would never have let him pass by without speaking. But the Andrew I knew would never have left me. I reread the note. I had smoothed it as best I could. No matter how disheartening, it was the last thing I received from my husband.

11

Scott Harrington

I skipped breakfast at St. John's to keep an early morning watch, determined that I wouldn't miss Tyler when he left the shelter. Seated on a corner bench diagonal to Three Rivers Missions, I hid behind the morning newspaper but kept looking over it, scanning the surrounding area. I'd been sitting there for about two hours now and couldn't possibly have missed him on my watch. The time on my phone showed nine in the morning. In the next thirty minutes, everyone had to be out.

But he didn't come. I waited past nine, nine thirty, ten. Somehow I'd missed him. My lookout had been diligent. The only possibilities were that he left before I arrived at seven or he didn't stay there last night.

My stomach knotted at the prospect of him doing another delivery tonight. Any one of them could lead to the cops busting him, or worse. But I had no idea where to find him. This place provided the only connection we had. What else could I do but be in the vicinity again late afternoon and wait some more?

At ten fifteen I headed home. This assignment wore me out physically and emotionally.

I hopped on a bus headed down the Ohio Valley toward Sewickley. I looked a mess, wrinkled and in need of a shower. I managed to blend in when I was in the city but stood out like an elephant on the highway in my little home town. Still, I risked offending people by stopping at Stella's.

I exited the bus a few doors down the street from the café. The twenty-minute ride had transported me to a different world. The shrubbery that bordered the sidewalk created their own miniature skyline of coned, rounded, and squared shrubbery in hues of green, crimson, and gold. Sapling trees interspersed the shrubs.

I entered the café and the rich aroma of coffee delighted my senses. Stella worked the counter by herself this morning. One customer sat sipping coffee, his eyes glued to a laptop. I caught the glance of distaste when I walked past.

"Hey, if it isn't Clark Kent. Welcome back to Metropolis. Man, are you a mess! Don't even think about hugging me." The tension of last night and this morning began to dissipate. Stella made the city seem so far away.

"Hi Stel." I could manage no more. My legs felt too heavy to move.

"Hey, did you run a marathon and come in last? What can I get for you?"

"Definitely coffee. I know it's almost lunch, but I haven't had breakfast. What's quick this morning?"

"Tell you what." She poured my coffee into a to-go cup. "Julie came in to cover the register, and I need to run home. How about you take your coffee and go get your shower—I hope that's your plan 'cause you need it. I'll package you up something good and drop it off in five. Here's a macadamia cookie to tide you over."

I took the coffee and the cookie. "Thanks, Stella.

You're the best."

She smiled. "You got that right. Don't forget it."

I was upstairs putting on some fresh clothes when I heard the doorbell, followed by the key turning. "It's me," Stella called. "And Ginger."

Ginger barreled up the stairs, her tail thumping the wall. I ruffled her fur, pulled on my shirt, and went barefoot down the stairs.

The net had been removed from Stella's clipped-up blond hair. She wore jeans and a neon-green polo shirt with *Stella's Café* on the pocket. She set a feast on my table. "This is for later. I'll put it in your fridge."

I recognized the box lunch that held one of her specialty sandwiches and a side or two.

I glanced in the to-go box she set before me to find a quiche and crispy potatoes. "What do I owe you?"

"On the house, my friend." She closed the refrigerator door and walked back toward the table.

"Stella, how do you make a living?"

"Hey, I'm doing OK. My car's bigger than your car. The real question is, how do you make a living with months between projects?" Her brows arched.

The corners of my mouth lifted into a grin. "A little trust fund helps. Do you have time to sit? I could use some normal company. There's enough food here for three of us."

She sat across from me. "You planning to set a place for Ginger? And what's with the glasses? I've never seen you wear them."

"I pulled out my contacts. Not a good idea to leave them in all night." I took a long, slow swallow of coffee, detecting a slight taste of hazelnut.

"Well, you look quite intelligent. Kind of sophisticated."

"That's not what they said in third grade."

She grimaced. "Ouch. Eight-year-olds can be cruel."

"Tell me about it. I got 'Four-eyes' and 'Specky' all the time. One day in second grade, we were leaving school and a kid, fooling around, acted like he couldn't see. He bumped into me and said, 'Sorry Speckles. Couldn't see you behind those goggles.' Edwin sprinted over and decked him. A teacher had to pull him off of the kid. I stood watching while one went to the nurse and the other to the office. Edwin had a three-day suspension."

I picked up the knife. "Half a quiche?"

"No. Just this." She took an orange scone from the bag and opened a little container of marmalade. I'd talked with her before about my project and shared a little about Pete, D.J., and Tyler, but not about the drugs. So I filled her in. "I waited for over three hours and didn't catch him. It's eating at me because I wanted to get him out of there."

"Scott, what are you planning? How do you get him out of that environment without offering him something different?" Stella could always read me.

I rubbed my temples and moved my head from side to side to relieve the stiffness. My hair was still damp from my shower.

She continued. "You're planning to bring him here, aren't you?"

I gave her a grin. "I've thought about it."

She wrinkled her brows. "You sure that's a good idea? You don't know this kid."

"What choice do I have? I feel like I know him. I think he's a good kid who's had some bad breaks."

"Let's not forget he's a drug trafficker. He knows

what he's doing."

She had a point. "Only because he's desperate. Take that away and...I don't know, Stel. Am I being foolish to think of this?"

Right now, her thoughts would be clearer than mine.

"You know, you can't save every stray dog that comes to your door." She refuted herself. "Bad analogy. I know this is more important than that. Just be careful. I could talk with Pastor Doug and see if he knows of any avenues for help? There must be places someone like him can go."

"Not yet. Let me think about it."

She glanced at the stack of magazines and DVDs that contained some past work I'd done. Stella would have been familiar with much of it. "What's with the nostalgia?"

"Going through to pick out a few things. I met a young lady at the offices of Three Rivers Missions and promised to bring some of my work to show her."

"Oh." Her arms crossed over her chest, and she stood to leave. "Gotta go. The deli's calling me. You can leave Ginger here. I'll pick her up on my way home." With that, she bolted out the door without any good-bye.

I had many things to do but couldn't be effective without a rest. I finished my food, set my phone alarm for one hour, and hit the sofa. Ginger hopped up and lay at my feet.

I woke rested and thankful for the blissful unconsciousness. What to do about Tyler? I went to my laptop and typed "Tyler Pulkowski" into a search engine. Three Tylers were pictured, but none were him. However, one link identified him as part of the graduating class from a Pittsburgh high school. I clicked to open it but only found school reports.

Tyler's name registered in the list of five-hundred other students. I narrowed my search to the Southside of Pittsburgh where Tyler said they lived before his dad left. That produced an obituary for Francis Pulkowski, survived by two sons, Francis, Jr. and Samuel Pulkowski and by four grandchildren who remained unnamed. I searched Francis and Samuel. Bingo. An article featured Sam Pulkowski leading a construction crew of volunteers rebuilding a home destroyed by fire. One picture featured Sam and his young son, Tyler, then about seven years old. Tyler's frame nestled close to Sam's leg, and Sam's hand rested on Tyler's crew cut.

Sam Pulkowski. I gazed at the picture. Print media can't show a person's character, but he sure didn't look like a dad who would leave his son behind. I'd love to hear his side of the story. He shouldn't be too difficult to find.

Refreshed and ready, I reached for the stack of articles I'd selected to show...or show off to Caroline. That's what was really happening here.

After stopping by Three Rivers offices, I would find Tyler. This time I'd take my car to the city—no bus, no ragged clothes, no backpack. After that, I'd bring Tyler home with me. I couldn't wait for Stella to talk with her pastor. She'd agree once she got to know him. I had enough connections that should help Tyler to secure a job. His time in my home would be short. It would be an easy sacrifice on my end.

Driving on I-279 into the city, a cold afternoon rain spattered against my windshield. I cursed at the thought of sitting on a wet bench for hours. I'd see

Caroline first.

I opened the office door to *déjà vu*. A spreadsheet stretched across Caroline's desk. She peeked over her glasses without a word, as she penciled something into the columns. *Remember, Harrington, rude, cute, snarky, sassy. First comes rude.* I proceeded to her desk and spoke, even though she had returned to her task.

"Hello, Carol-line."

"Oh, hi. It's the newspaper guy."

"Or it's the journalist."

"You like to make a big deal out of that, don't you?" She pointed her pencil at me.

"Well, the newspaper guy could be the one throwing them on the porch from a bicycle. He could be the one doing the print setting. Could be the person..."

"OK, OK. I get it. What can I do for you today?"

"Well, two things. First, I brought some articles I wrote in the past so you can scan my work. I'm sure you'll want to know you're being represented well." That caught her attention.

"Oh yeah, you said you'd be doing that. Pull that chair on over so you can tell me what I'm looking at."

I found my cold metal chair and brought it to her desk, placing it along the side rather than across from her. I knew this work inside out but would rather not be looking at it upside down.

As I sat beside her, she closed the cover of her spreadsheet.

"Quite old school, doing paper and pencil. Excel can handle that for you."

Strawberry-blond eyebrows raised over her glasses. "Well, why didn't I think of that?" Her voice dripped with sarcasm. She slid the spreadsheet in the middle drawer of her desk and turned back with a smile. "So, let's see what you've done, Mr. Harrington."

This girl could change like a chameleon.

"Scott," I reminded her.

For the next hour, we flipped through some of my work. Caroline pulled out the Pittsburgh travelogue I'd done two years ago. It had won an award, but only for a local magazine, nothing too prestigious.

"So, walk me through Pittsburgh," she requested.

The clock in my sights said three twenty and as much as I would've liked to stick around, I had resolved to be out the door by three forty. I couldn't let Tyler down. I decided to play her game.

"I've got twenty minutes. Do you want a quick overview or shall I focus on one or two places?"

"Well, I certainly don't want to keep you from something more important, Mr. Harrington." Snippy returned, and it made me smile.

"No problem at all. I'll start at the beginning and keep moving. If something catches your fancy, we'll slow down."

We didn't get too far before Phipps Conservatory and Botanical Gardens caught her eye.

"That reminds me of the gardens behind my home in Savannah. Look, there's a Camellia. They bloom in the spring and in the winter. Oh, a magnolia. That, my friend, is a real magnolia, not one of the poor imitations you have up here in the north. Crepe myrtle. Ahh. I haven't seen one of those in way too long."

Her eyes had a genuine glow I hadn't seen before. Nostalgia. She missed Savannah.

With her hand covering the foliage, she inhaled. "I can almost smell it. Where is this place? I want to go there."

Somewhat amused, I grinned. "It's in Schenley Park."

"And where exactly is that?" Why did her question sound like a commanding officer?

"It's at...never mind. I'll take you there. One o'clock Saturday afternoon?"

She pulled her glasses to the tip of her nose and turned to study me. I'd never seen her speechless except when she should be greeting visitors in the office.

Her answer came with arched brows. "So, no lunch first?"

"OK, Miss Savannah, Georgia—noon. Where shall I pick you up?"

"Oh, I'll meet you." She riffled back a few pages and pointed. "At this place."

The Wellford Lounge on the overlook at Mount Washington. The girl had good taste.

The clock read three forty-five. "Gotta go. I'll meet you at the Wellford Lounge at noon on Saturday."

A wide smile. "Oh, you said there were two things you wanted today."

I had to think for a minute. "Oh yeah, I wanted to see if I could meet Ray Brockman. But I'm tight on time. Some other day."

"Has to be. He's not in anyway."

I opened the door to exit but turned toward her once again.

"Hey, one final question. Do you know if there's much drug activity around the Three Rivers Mission on Stanwix?"

Caroline leaned back in her chair and crossed her legs. Her chin tipped upward. "It's a homeless shelter.

I would imagine some of those men are junkies."

I started to clarify my question but decided to let it drop. "Yeah, you're right."

She furrowed her brows. "So why the question?"

No way would I mention Tyler. "I want to keep it out of my story."

"Good plan. I'll see you Saturday."

12

Scott Harrington

I was determined to find Tyler before he went to the shelter. Carnegie Library had branches throughout the Pittsburgh area, but only the Smithfield Street branch was downtown. That must be where Tyler spent his days.

Approaching the library, I glanced up at the colorful mural, *The Two Andys*, painted on the side of a building. Andy Warhol and Andrew Carnegie depicted in a beauty parlor displayed the artists' attempt to symbolize a revitalized city.

I entered the library and began scanning the rows of bookshelves. There was no sign of Tyler. He had said he used the computers to check e-mail, so I made my way to the database center. He wasn't there.

I left the library and turned toward Stanwix Street. The shelter wouldn't be open yet, but I'd keep walking back and forth. Eventually, I'd find him somewhere between these two places.

As I turned a corner, I caught sight of his lanky frame and wheat-colored hair in the distance. I'd have to sprint to catch up with him.

I picked up my pace but slowed as I saw Jim lumbering toward Tyler, his shoulders held tight with fisted hands. When he reached Tyler, he jabbed a finger in his chest. They were too far away to hear their conversation, but Jim stepped close to Tyler, face-to-face. Tyler's attempt to inch back was futile as Jim stepped in again, wrapping a huge hand around Tyler's arm. A few more words were exchanged. Then Jim pointed his finger toward his face before pivoting around. As he walked away, Tyler leaned over, hands on his thighs.

I approached, watching for any return of Jim. When I stood behind him, close enough to touch, I laid a hand on his shoulder. "You OK?"

I hadn't intended to startle him, but he jumped at my touch. "Scott." He let out a relieved breath, his eyes darting in the direction where Jim had just walked.

I motioned in the opposite direction. "Let's get out of here."

This time, he didn't argue. He fell into step beside me, and we walked. Pedestrian traffic was thick. Meandering away from the crowds, we ended up under the bridge where I slept that first night. With the place unoccupied now, we leaned against the massive pillars imbedded in a concrete foundation.

Daytime sounded so different, with the constant swoosh of cars passing above like a pulsing heartbeat. Brakes squealed and a distant siren beat out a series of high and low tones. But the dampness and trash were the same, as though they were rooted under this bridge. I shuddered from the memory of sleeping here.

Tyler shut his eyes, exhaling deep breaths. The emotional fatigue was evident.

I silently watched him for a few minutes. "You OK?"

"Yeah, I'm OK. I was looking for you." His

breathing returned to normal.

"Well, that makes two of us. I was looking for you as well."

"You looking so you could tell me how much trouble I was getting in? To say 'I told you so'? Well, too late. I figured that one out." He glanced from side-to-side.

I shook my head. "No, I was looking because I'm worried about you. Jim's trying his best to intimidate you. What did he say?"

Tyler moved from the concrete pylons and sat on a railroad tie. "I didn't stay at the shelter last night. He came looking for me to find out why."

"Did he threaten you?"

He gave a half-shrug. "He wanted to make sure I'm still in. The threat was implied if I'd have answered differently."

I leaned back and folded my hands in front of my chest. "So you're still going to work for him?"

"No, but I'm not stupid enough to tell him that. I had a bad scare last night. I've got to get out."

I unfolded my arms and sat on the cold ground, facing him. "What happened?"

Tyler slid his backpack off and looped his foot through the straps. "I took the West End Bridge to Carson Street just like he instructed me. I found the row house, but no one waited outside, so I parked at the curb and hung around for a few minutes, not knowing what else to do. Finally, I walked to the door and rang the bell."

Tyler rested his elbows on his knees, his hands clasped under his chin. "There was no answer. Went back to the car to check my address. I had the right place. I was sure I walked into a bust. My hands went clammy, and I fumbled putting the key in the ignition. All of a sudden there was a thwack on my window. It almost gave me a heart attack."

He sat up straight, an involuntary spasm twitching his face. "I couldn't see the face in the dark. I didn't know if it was my contact or the cops. My hand shook so bad I could barely roll the window down. When I did, I saw the man described on my paper. I made the exchange and couldn't get out of there fast enough."

I nodded. "So do you have a plan?"

"I'm getting outta here. I gotta go as far as I can from this city. There's nothing here for me but trouble." He raised his head arching one brow. "Winter's coming. You have any interest in heading someplace warmer?"

I stood and leaned against the pylon, tapping my fingers together. "Ty, I think there's another way. I think we should go to the police."

He rose to his feet, hands on his hips. "Are you crazy? No way am I going to the cops. You know what I've been doing. They'll lock me up."

"No, they won't. They won't want you. You've been a pawn, used in a bigger game. They want the game master." I took a few steps toward him. "Listen Ty, did they ever tell you what the packages held?"

"No, but…"

"No." My hand swept down, closing my fist like a conductor halting the music. "That's all. No but's, just no. You tell the police you weren't aware. When you became suspicious, you stopped and went to the authorities."

"Yeah. Then I'm a dead man." A siren above sounded, as if in confirmation.

I stepped toward him. "They'll protect you. We'll

tell them you need protection."

He shook his head. "I'm not doing it, Scott. Why should I? I can walk away if I get outta this city."

"Yeah, you walk away and kids all over Pittsburgh are shooting poison in their arms, dying at sixteen. Can you live with that?" My forward motion brought me right before him.

Tyler turned his head away. "Why did I want to find you anyway? You always judge me."

I stepped back and ran my hands through my hair. Walking back toward the bridge support, I braced my arms and head against the pitted metal pillar.

"Sorry, Scott. I don't mean to sound heartless, but they're kids that choose it. No one makes them use drugs. I can't stop it. It's a bigger problem than I can fix."

My shoulders slumped with the heaviness. My tone became more of a plea. "What if you could stop it for one kid? Would that be worth the risk?"

He lowered his head avoiding my eyes. "Can't."

"You mean won't." I spit out the word with emphasis.

Tyler stiffened. "Judging me again." He started walking away from the damp, musty overpass.

"Hey wait, Ty. I need to tell you some things. Need to tell you why this is so important to me."

"You can tell me, but I'm not going to the police. I'm hopping on a Greyhound, and I won't look back."

13

Scott Harrington

I sat on a landscaping tie and Tyler joined me. Telling Tyler my brother OD'd would be insufficient. I needed him to see Edwin, to see us as kids, to know the cost. Taking a deep breath, I pictured Edwin in my mind. My occupation depended on using words to make people real. I needed that skill right now.

"Edwin was a year older than me—fourteen months to be exact. When we were young, we only had each other. No neighborhood kids or friends to invite over. Just him and me. We were typical boys—we wrestled, played ball, video games. Our parents were rarely around. Leticia, our nanny, raised us. Sometimes our mother would take us to the country club with her, and we'd swim with the other kids."

Tyler's eyebrows rose.

I ignored it. "I don't think she wanted to take us, but her socialite friends took their kids. She had to keep up appearances. We lived in an impressive old house, my dad's family home for two generations back."

I left it at that for Tyler's sake. He grew up in poverty. It would be cruel to describe the long entrance lined with trees, the fountain at the bend in the governor's driveway, and the huge pillars towering the front of the 17,000 square-foot house. He already surmised that we were wealthy.

"I never knew anything else until high school. Then I realized everyone didn't live like that."

Tyler eyed my frayed jeans.

"Might sound impressive, but believe me, for two boys growing up with absent parents and no other friends, we couldn't have cared less. Most of the house remained off limits to us anyway. In many ways, Edwin and I just had each other." I stood and paced for a moment.

Tyler sat there, waiting for the rest of my story. The wind picked up and a few leaves from the grassy embankment blew past.

"Hormones hit him like an eighteen-wheeler. I didn't recognize it at the time, but looking back, I can see it. It seemed like all of a sudden, he shut me out, not wanting to do anything together. At fifteen, he starting hanging with the cool kids from school. I wasn't cool by anyone's standard—skinny, awkward, and wearing glasses. I guess kids today might call me dorky. Dorky and quiet. I didn't talk much to anyone but Edwin."

Tyler didn't interject. Was he starting to see beyond his belief that these are kids that choose drugs? There are always circumstances—something they're searching for.

"He started sneaking out when he should have been in bed. A couple of times, I woke and went in to talk. He seemed spacy, and I figured he'd been drinking. One night, I went looking for a CD he had used. I went in his bedroom and checked in his nightstand drawer. I found needles and some white stuff. I knew it had to be drugs. I couldn't stop fretting about it. The next day I told him I had seen the drugs. He lunged at me and pushed me up against the wall, his arm pressed into my neck. He told me if I said one word, he'd beat the crap outta me, but his language came out a little stronger. I asked him what it was. He said, 'Heroin. And don't you ever touch it.'

"I spent the next three months knowing and not doing anything about it. I watched him kill himself, but I remained quiet. I should've gone to my dad, or at least to Leticia. But—and believe me, I know how stupid this sounds—I didn't want Edwin to get mad at me. A month after his sixteenth birthday, they found him under the bleachers at the school's football field, dead from an overdose."

Tyler said nothing.

"You know, Ty, you said these kids choose it. But I want you to think about this. We weren't raised in a normal home. No dad to throw ball or mom to tuck us in. Edwin was searching, but he didn't know what for."

Tyler gazed at me, unblinking. "I hear what you're saying, but I didn't have a normal home. No mom or dad to show any support. I've been searching for something all my life. But I didn't take drugs."

I bit back the words, *but you sold them*. That wouldn't help me get my point across. A better way was if I just sat down and continued my story.

"After that, my family went crazy. Dad raged and wanted to find someone to blame and bring to justice. Mom blamed my dad because he didn't spend any time with us. Next thing I knew, they filed for divorce. Dad got the house, which had been in his family, and cursed about not having a pre-nup. Mom got me and a multi-million-dollar settlement. Leticia got a severance package. My mother moved me to Scarsdale. After that, I only saw my dad once or twice a year.

"At eighteen, I headed for Columbia University. They were horrified that I planned to study journalism and not law. I don't think Dad has forgiven me yet. He had lost his golden boy. We all knew it. My dad always talked about the day when the firm would be Harrington and Harrington."

I stood again and stretched my cramped legs, too tall to sit like that for long.

"They didn't know I could have stepped up to the plate and helped my brother. Instead, I sat back and watched him destroy himself. I live with guilt every day of my life. It about destroyed me the first year after he died."

I returned to my seat. "So, Ty, that's why I can't walk away from this. Someone has a brother, a son, a best friend who needs help. I am going to the police. The only question is whether you'll go with me."

Tyler knitted his brows. "So, if your family's so rich, why are you out here?"

"A whole different story, buddy. Let's stick with the police for now. Will you do it?"

He ran both hands through his hair before cradling his head in hands. "Here's what I'll do. I got no place to go. Can't go back to Three Rivers Mission, and I can't go back to sleeping under this bridge. I'm headed somewhere away from this city. I'll go with you, and then I'm gone. From the police to the bus station. That's all I can do."

I couldn't let it go at that. The officers would want to follow up. And the documentary—Tyler's might be the best piece. I could write it without his consent if I didn't use his name or any specifics that would identify him. That would diminish the story's impact.

Besides, if he left for another state, he'd still be without a home. I didn't put myself on the line for my brother. I'd like to think I outgrew that selfishness.

"What if I could help you stay here?"

Tyler shook his head as though clearing the cobwebs from his brain. "Why do you think you can help me when you can't help yourself?"

The time had come. I wouldn't be any benefit to Tyler without breaking my cover.

"Here's the scoop. There is a part of the story I told you that you may have missed. Remember I said I went off to Columbia? They have about the best journalism school around. Well, that's what I do, the reason I'm here."

Tyler still seemed confused, but then understanding seemed to settle in his brain. His mouth went slack as his eyes widened. "You...you're a writer?" His voice rose, stuttering. "That's why you're here? To get a story?"

"Yeah, but hear me out."

He sprang to his feet, hands clenched tight. "And why should I hear you out? You lied and used people for your own purposes. Am I in that book?"

He backed away from me.

I stood and took a few steps to join him. "It's not a book, Ty. Listen. I'm trying to do some good work here."

"How self-sacrificing." He nodded in mock agreement, his sarcasm wrapping around me like a straightjacket. "You wanna get some pictures? I could lay down here with my backpack if you have a camera."

"Tyler. Listen. It's not like that. I'm hoping to..." I

couldn't finish my sentence. I hoped to win an award. That was the bottom line. Yet, I still felt the story needed to be told.

I tried again. "Most people don't know what it's like to be without a home. I want to bring awareness that these are real people in real trouble. How are we helping and what more can we do? I think it's something people need to hear."

He clenched his fists. "Well, put this in your story."

After making an obscene hand gesture, he took off.

I watched his departing back for a brief moment before I called after him. "Can we talk about this?" When he kept walking, I made a snap decision and called again. "I have an extra bedroom."

That stopped him in his tracks, but he didn't turn around.

"I have connections that can get you a job."

That made the difference. He turned around and took slow steps back toward me.

"In exchange for my story?"

"Nope. No conditions. But if you agree, I'd like to write your story."

"And if I don't agree?"

"Your decision. All I ask is that you give me a chance to show you what I'm doing."

"If I agree, no pictures, no name." He crossed his hands over his chest, head back and chin jutted forward, a mix of pride and desperation.

I nodded. "I can work with that."

It would have to be enough for now. I would convince him later.

His eyes fixed on mine, the anger still evident. "How long can I stay?"

"Let's get you off the street before we work out all the details, OK?"

Tyler uncrossed his arms and nodded, still miffed at me, but we were making steps.

"Let's get out of here, go home, and get cleaned up. We'll get a good meal from Stella, before we come in to the police station."

"Who's Stella—your wife?"

"Nah. Stella's my neighbor, and she runs a little café. Good food. Good lady."

"She your girlfriend?"

"Nope. The girl next door—literally."

~*~

I turned into my driveway, Tyler in the passenger seat. Nothing like my childhood home, the simple two-story clapboard painted a discreet ivory, sat on a quiet street. The houses were built with a few feet between them and fronted by sidewalks.

I pointed at the house to the right of mine. "That's where Stella lives. You'll get to know her well." I motioned toward the corner intersection. "Church Street. The café is down there and around the corner."

When we entered the house, Tyler gazed, wide-eyed. He turned around, his eyes darting everywhere in my little home. "Wow."

"Let me show you around." I motioned toward each area. "The living room, dining room, and kitchen sort of run together." We walked past the half-wall that divided the kitchen, and I opened the door to the patio.

"This is fenced so Ginger can run without her leash. Oh, you haven't met the old girl. She's next door at Stella's. She keeps her if I'm going to be out too long to leave her alone. Come on back inside. I'll show you your bedroom."

We stepped back inside and started up the stairs. I scanned the house with new eyes, seeing things I took for granted. The weekly cleaning service kept it in good order. Hardwood floors shined to a glowing finish, the hexagon window at the curve of the stairs scattered light on the landing.

"The first room on the right is mine and the one across from it is where you'll stay. The third bedroom down the hall is overflow. I keep it for an office but mostly work at the dining room table anyway."

We stepped into Tyler's room, no frills, a definite masculine décor, but spacious enough for a queen-sized sleigh bed and a chest of drawers. The heavy, well-built pine furniture glowed with a rich, dark wood tone.

"Sorry there's no TV in here." I opened the closet, where one side remained empty for the rare occasion when I had a house guest. "You can keep your things in here."

Tyler's mouth fell open, disbelief etched on his face as he touched the smooth wooden surfaces and stroked the comforter on the bed. "Man, this is nice. And this is just for company?"

"Not anymore. Now it's for you."

I sorted through my closet while Tyler took a long shower. Although his backpack bulged, it didn't hold much of value. Both taller and fuller than Ty's thin frame, my jeans would never work. But he could get by with some of my T-shirts. I pulled out three of them, as well as clean socks. I would do a department store run and pick up some faded jeans, let him think those were my old ones that no longer fit.

But first, we had to eat. I called Stella's to order takeout. She answered the café phone herself.

"Hey, Stel, It's Scott."

"You home?"

"Yep. Didn't get Ginger yet, but I want to place an order. I'll run over and pick it up."

"You want the special? It's Chicken Pesto Panini with a beet salad."

"Yeah, minus the beet salad. Make it a Caesar salad, and make that two orders."

"Two orders of salad, or two orders of everything?"

"Everything."

"Got company, or are you extraordinarily hungry today? And what's wrong with my beet salad?"

Ignoring the other questions, I replied, "Love your Caesar's. I'll be there in ten minutes."

Always throw her a food compliment.

"Don't bother. I'm bringing it over."

I grinned and shook my head. She couldn't stand not knowing.

Tyler looked fresh with his hair damp and combed back, disguising the chopped haircut. My navy-blue pocket-T fit him well. No one would perceive anything but a clean-cut kid. That's what I wanted Stella to see.

The doorbell rang before Stella walked in.

"Delivery," she called. She came to the table and pulled out a myriad of small containers—Panini, Caesar, and beet salads, two of each.

I raised my eyes to question when I saw the beet salads.

"Don't judge it 'til you try it." She looked around for another person.

"Tyler." I mouthed it without sound then walked to the stairs and called. "Hey, Tyler. Dinner's here."

He came down the stairs, and I introduced him to Stella.

"I'm pleased to meet you, Tyler. Scott's told me about you."

His shoulders slumped, and he avoided eye contact. "Oh? What did he tell you?"

Stella walked toward him and thrust out her hand, making him raise his gaze. "He told me he met a very nice kid."

Tyler let out a huge breath and shook her hand. "Yeah, I appreciate his help. Thanks for bringing this over."

"You're welcome. Hope you like it."

His eyes lit as he glanced at the open cartons. "Are those beets? I haven't had beets for a long time."

Stella jutted up her chin and raised her eyebrows as she shot a smug glance in my direction. "It's a beet salad with pears, almonds, and goat cheese."

"Awesome."

That's all it took for him to win Stella over. All other indiscretions would be forgiven.

14

Claire Bassett

It wasn't possible.

Jason had seen someone who resembled Andrew and had imagined it to be him. I succinctly put it out of my mind every time it entered. I had to dismiss that possibility. There was no chance that Jason wouldn't be certain if it had been Andrew.

Dressing for my evening with Jonathan, I chose my clothing with care. Nothing that would appear like I tried to impress. Dress slacks, a simple sweater, and a scarf to enhance it. I didn't know the restaurant where we were headed, but he said casual.

I glanced in the mirror, again struck by the difference in my reflection from the days before tragedy visited us. The highlights in my hair left a glow that embraced my face with the smooth, angled cut, classy and sophisticated—everything that I was not. The look belonged to my mother. I always admired her refined countenance but didn't share it. I looked good, but artificial, and that brought a sadness to my face.

I gave my parents one last thank you and instructions for bedtime routines.

Mom smiled. "Claire, you look stunning. I always knew you had suppressed beauty."

A back-handed compliment if I ever heard one. The hidden meaning? She had to be the one to choose my clothes and hairstyle to get it done correctly. But I had to let it go. They were so good to me.

I kissed Drew and Isabella and closed the door behind me, fighting the nerves that churned my stomach.

Gauging from his look, Jonathan must have thought I looked stunning, too. He waited outside of Dante's House when I walked from the parking lot. A warmth rose to my cheeks at the caress in his eyes. His gaze didn't break, even as I stood before him. My hands moistened with a heat that flushed my skin. Without any touch, it became an intimate moment, unnerving me and reminding me I needed to talk about boundaries. But that would have been an intrusion into a moment so special. I returned his gaze until his hand took mine and we walked inside.

Dante's was a well-kept secret, about twenty minutes south of Slippery Rock. A romantic setting, lit by candles, it featured live music from a piano, guitar, and vocalist. A soothing tune of "Where is the Love?" hummed through the speakers in harmony.

I stared, taking in the beauty. "How did you find this place? It's incredible."

"Investigative detective work. I figured I had to impress you if I want there to be a second time."

"Jonathan," I began to protest. But he placed a silencing finger close to my lips.

"Sorry. Let's enjoy tonight."

A hostess escorted us to our table where Jonathan pulled out my chair. He sat to my right rather than across from me. It did make conversation easier, but the nearness both warmed me and frightened me. I became far too vulnerable in this man's presence.

A waiter filled our water goblets and inquired about our drinks. Turning toward me, Jonathan asked, "How's Argentina Merlot?"

Not a wine connoisseur, I knew little distinction beyond red or white. I nodded my agreement.

"We'd like a carafe of Zuccardi's." He assured me I would love it. Looking at the genuine Italian menu, he began, with intentional humor, to decimate the names on the menu. They were authentic, and he spoke them with a harsh staccato so different from the fluid beauty of the Italian language. I laughed until the waiter returned with our wine.

The food came out to perfection, both taste and presentation. My chicken fricassee was fork tender, with crisp, parmesan edges and oven-roasted vegetables. Jonathan ordered linguine *di mare*, scooping a small taste onto my plate. The tangy sauce awakened my taste buds. Soft music created a surreal atmosphere with familiar tunes crooned by new voices: "Bridge Over Troubled Water," "In the Still of the Night," "Can You Feel the Love Tonight?" Music of romance. The whole evening swept me into a new world. The wine, the music, the atmosphere. And his eyes. Jonathan's gaze stayed fixed on me all through dinner. When our plates were removed, he sought my hand and held it in his with the tenderness of a freshly plucked rose.

After we ate, we walked hand in hand to the lake behind the restaurant. Jonathan stopped by his car to retrieve his camera.

"I brought a night lens. Let's see what we can capture."

My untrained eye saw only darkness ahead, but

Jonathan seemed excited about something.

"Look at the stars. This will make an awesome shot."

I still didn't see it, but he aimed, focused, refocused, and snapped a series of pictures. After setting the camera for review, he pulled them up in a tiny window. I gasped as I saw the millions of stars polka-dotting the black sky. On some, there were radiant light beams. On others, the formation of constellations was discernible. Even the thumbnail viewer displayed the beauty.

"Stand over there. No, on second thought, sit on the bench."

I moved to the bench on a path to the lake's dock. It sat on an arched overpass not more than six-feet long spanning the rivulets of water jutting into land. Jonathan's camera snapped rapid-fire shots until I held my hand up, laughing.

"Stop. Enough of me."

He snapped me laughing, walking back toward him, and with my hands rising to cover the lens. Only then did he turn the camera off and allowed it to dangle from the strap around his neck. With his hands free, he caught both of mine, raised them to his lips and kissed each hand. Caught between laughter and surprise, my effort to pull them away held little protest. Jonathan shifted my hands and drew me toward him, stretching my arms over his shoulders and around his neck. I began to pull back, but he held me, firm yet soft.

"I won't hurt you, Claire."

"I know." I couldn't manage more than that whispered response. He placed the gentlest of kisses on my lips. I wanted to lean into him and welcome the kiss. But I couldn't. Guilt and desire battled until guilt overshadowed. I allowed the kiss, but I couldn't encourage more. I pulled back.

He released me, capturing my hand.

"Was that so bad?" His words teased, but his voice cracked with emotion.

I touched his face with my free hand. "No, Jonathan. It was sweet. But it's all I can do."

"It's all I'll ask…for now."

We walked to my car where he again leaned in and placed a gentle kiss on my cheek. I drove home realizing I never approached the topic of boundaries. We had already stepped over the ones my mind had established.

~*~

Monday morning, I walked to my desk. As I pulled out my chair, it contained a gold, nine-by-eleven mailing envelope, sealed only by the brass fastener. I smiled as I pulled out pictures of myself sitting, laughing, and walking. They were incredible pictures. I'd ask him later how many terrible shots had to be discarded to capture these. My favorite showed a darkened sky over a rippled lake with a vast display of stars bringing it all to light. A simple post-it note said, "You brought light into my darkness."

I smiled at his words and then reached to drop the note in the trash. On second thought, I opened my drawer, moved the pencil tray, paper clips, and stapler aside, and stuck it far in the back. No matter the circumstance, when a woman is abandoned by her husband, she's left to feel undesirable. When the pain of rejection threatened to consume me, I would steal a glance at my little yellow three-by-three square.

15

Scott Harrington

I felt sure of myself when we talked under the bridge, but uncertainty crept in, making me doubt my own words. Tyler had been delivering. All of a sudden, I questioned my guarantee that it would be dismissed. I needed to get some advice before I put him at risk. The thought of calling my father filled me with tension. I rubbed the stiffness in my neck, turned it from side to side trying to ease the taunt muscles, then picked up my phone and dialed.

A mixture of emotions came with his voice. The booming tones always spoke of his level of command, shrinking my confidence. The contrasting emotion was relief that I had reached his voice mail. I didn't leave a message. He'd see a missed call, but I doubted he would return it.

Hitting the keys on my laptop, I found another phone number and called a local attorney. He would see us in one hour. *It's only money, Harrington.*

Lawrence Greene agreed to accompany us to the police station. We would share nothing until we had a signed immunity for Tyler. We reached him on a slow day and would go directly to the precinct. He would drive himself and meet us there.

I pulled the car into an open parking space in the

lot behind the station. Tyler's eyes darted back and forth, scanning the area. He placed a baseball cap on his head and gave the visor a final tug to shield his eyes.

I stifled a smile. "Hey, buddy, can't get much safer than the police station."

"I don't need anyone to see me going in here. Or you, for that matter. They see you, they'll figure I'm the one under the hat. Jim probably has his goons all over the city looking for me. By now, he knows I bolted."

Tyler opened the passenger door and took off. I had to sprint from the car to the building to keep up with him.

Stepping inside the outer lobby, a tiny space with a half-wall separated us from the uniformed officer at the desk. Safety glass furthered the accessibility. Pamphlets, brochures, and folded maps were displayed on plastic wall-mounted bins for the public to help themselves.

Where was Greene? I couldn't start this without him.

The officer spoke through the safety glass. "What's your business today?"

"Um … We're waiting for one other person to join us."

"Well, you can't wait in here. State your business, or you'll have to be on your way."

As he spoke, the door opened, and the attorney walked in. He marched to the window and took charge.

"We need to see a detective, please. Is Paul Everson available?"

"No, sir, but I can get you someone else. Adam Fulton is here."

Sir? We almost got the boot, but he got a "Sir."

"That'll do."

The officer picked up the phone and pushed a single button.

"Is Fulton back there?" He paused, listening before he continued. "OK. When he's off the phone, send him out." He hung up the phone and turned back to the window, motioning us to the bench. "Have a seat. Someone'll see you soon."

Turning, I could see the height markings on the doorframe. Tyler scooted to the far end of the bench, out of view of the window. Twenty minutes passed before a plain-clothes officer came to get us. The rectangular gold pin on his pocket said, "Detective Fulton."

"Adam Fulton," he introduced himself. What can I do for you today?"

We all stood but, as advised, Tyler and I remained silent.

Lawrence Greene asked for somewhere private where we could discuss a possible crime.

He turned and nodded to the uniformed officer. "I'm bringing 'em back."

That set the desk officer in motion toward the side door that Detective Fulton had used. He opened it, requiring us to empty our pockets and walk through a scanner, confiscating our cell phones and my pocket knife until we were ready to leave.

The precinct room at the end of the hallway was filled with activity and cubicles. But we stopped short of that and were escorted to a small area that said "Processing" on the door. The uniformed officer handed Fulton a stack of papers and went back to the front desk.

Seated at a small table, he got right to business.

"So, what do you think you know?" He shuffled through the papers, looking for the one he needed.

"I have a client who has strong suspicion of a drug ring," Greene took charge. "He assisted without knowledge, receiving minimum compensation to make deliveries without awareness of the contents inside the packages. He has become suspicious and would like to report it. However, before that occurs, we need assurance that he won't be held culpable for that which he had no knowledge."

Fulton's eyes turned toward me and then to Tyler. "Are one of these men your client?"

"I can't discuss my client relationship until I have the requested assurance."

Fulton sat back, crossed his leg over one knee. "If what you're telling me is true, he won't be held accountable. If we determine that he knew what went down and gained from his involvement, that's another story."

Greene scratched his head. "Hmm. Well that leaves us at loggerheads. What's your criteria for determination?"

Fulton leaned back, his fingers interlocked behind his head. "Q&A."

Greene sighed. "This is most unfortunate. It could have been a major lead for you, filled with information. Thank you, and have a good day."

With that he stood and motioned for us to do likewise.

"Hold on. Sit down. I said if you're telling the truth, if he had no knowledge, he won't be charged."

I glanced at Tyler who had lost all color in his complexion.

Greene appeared to think it over and sat down. "I've drafted an immunity agreement. Please read it, and if you agree to sign it, you won't be sorry."

Fulton glanced at the paper. "There's no name here?"

"It has my client number and the name will be completed upon your signature."

Fulton reached into his shirt pocket, pulled out a pen, and scribbled his name. Greene held his hand out for the pen, inserted Tyler's name, separated the duplicate, and handed it to Detective Fulton. He folded the original and returned it to his briefcase.

"Detective Fulton, I'd like you to meet my client, Tyler Pulkowski. He's accompanied by a friend, Scott Harrington. I'll remain present for your questioning."

Money well spent.

After an hour of questions, Tyler had shared his experience with the shelter. He discussed meeting Jim, and he gave detailed descriptions of the places and people receiving deliveries. I proved to be an unnecessary fifth wheel, only sharing how I had met Tyler and our conversations about his involvement.

"We believe Tyler is at risk here and want to see what security you might be able to offer."

Fulton shook his head. "Lay low for a while. Keep away from the area. Did you find a place to stay?"

A sigh escaped as Tyler ran his hand through his hair. "Yeah."

I turned toward the officer. "What can we do to help?"

"Leave us your contact. We're going to put an undercover in there. If we need to talk to you again, we'll call."

"How will we know when this is over?" He stood

up even as I spoke.

"Watch the news." He walked to the door and motioned for the officer at the front desk.

"I'll be staying on top of this," Lawrence Greene interjected, speaking to Tyler.

He handed his card to the detective as the uniformed officer arrived to show us out.

~*~

I'd made a commitment to take Caroline to Phipps Conservatory and Botanical Gardens, but that meant leaving Tyler alone at my place.

He sat on the floor, playing with Ginger, using a knotted rope that served as a tug-of-war. "Hey, Ty, I have a lunch date and a tour to do today. You OK here for a while?"

He glanced up. "Yeah, I won't steal the silverware."

I sighed with a shake of my head. "That's not what I meant. I don't want to leave you feeling anxious about the whole situation."

"No, I'm OK. I don't feel threatened here. It's far enough away from town." He gave the rope a pull and Ginger held tight, shaking her head back and forth. "And I have this girl to protect me."

Tyler let the rope go free, ruffled Ginger's fur, and stood up. "But I don't have anything to do without a job. I can't keep mooching off of you. I've got to pay you back for that lawyer. How much is that gonna be?"

"You're not mooching. It's not costing me anything but a little food, and Stella keeps us well fed. Don't worry about the attorney. I've got that."

"How much is that? I can't let you pay to keep me outta trouble."

"Tyler, you're eighteen years old. You don't need to be worrying about legal fees." He stared at me in disbelief. Had no one ever taken care of him before?

"Thanks, Scott. I'll make it up to you. I promise."

"Relax. Watch some TV. You might find some college football."

"You got anything I can read?"

I had forgotten the kid was a book lover. "Sure. Help yourself. There's a shelf full of books in my bedroom."

~*~

I was about to give up on Miss Savannah, Georgia, when she arrived at twelve twenty. I caught a glimpse of her strawberry-blond hair stepping out of a sporty coupe. I couldn't make out the model, but it looked flashy and expensive. Not too shabby for a non-profit receptionist. Must have some of Daddy's money flowing up from Savannah.

She walked toward me, arms swinging and hips swaying, showing off the long legs her skirt did little to cover.

"Car trouble?"

"Excuse me?"

I tapped my watch. "You're late."

She glanced at the face of my watch. "Only twenty minutes." She put her arm through mine. "I'm starving."

We headed in to our table.

The Mount Washington Restaurant sat high atop a

cliff with a perfect view of the city, all of the tables positioned near the glass front. The fountain marked the spot where the three rivers met at the point. Our seats offered a clear view of the Duquesne Incline as the red trolley car made its slow journey up the tracks.

I might have expected a little admiration for the grandeur of the restaurant, but Caroline displayed nonchalance. She didn't seem to notice the crystal chandeliers, the fine china, or the incredible view. She walked right in without a word, apparently indifferent to the opulence. She didn't thank the waiter when he pulled out her chair. I offered a *thank you* on her behalf. Once seated, I eased into a chat about Three Rivers Mission. Still a journalist, I wouldn't miss an opportunity to gather information.

"So, tell me about Ray Brockman. He's rather elusive—never there when I am."

Her lips drew together in a smirk. "Not much when I am either. Let's say, he likes his flexibility."

"Well, does he ever come in?"

"Oh, sure. An hour here and there. I pretty much run things there. He poses that as a compliment—'oh you're so competent. I feel like I can take a little time for the family.' But I know better. Take a little time for the girlfriend is more like it." The more she spoke, the more her vowels elongated.

I sat back, enjoying the show. "I take it you aren't a Ray Brockman fan?"

"You think? Leaves me to the job of running three facilities for twenty-six thou a year? Job responsibilities of a CEO, salary of a receptionist. Can't even boast a better job title on a resume."

I couldn't resist a smile.

Her arms crossed in front of her. "What's so

funny? I'm not amused by any of that."

"Nothing. Let's order." This might be the quirkiest lunch date I'd ever had.

Our waiter approached the table, and Caroline called out her order. "Chilean Sea Bass without the cream glaze, a Caprese salad, balsamic on the side, and the almond brie appetizer to start." She lifted her menu with a detached demeanor and held it up to our waiter without making eye contact. Caroline McMann must have assumed a class distinction.

I was still processing the menu items but, once again, attempted to counter her rudeness with appreciation. "Excellent menu. How's the roast duck? Would you recommend that or the salmon?"

After hearing his detailed description, I thanked him and ordered the duck.

While we ate, I ventured again into the topic of Three Rivers Missions.

"So, you have a lot of responsibility to keep the shelters afloat. Do the directors report to you?"

"Not officially, but in reality, yes. When they want something, they call me. I do all of their ordering and pay the invoices. Each director oversees their own employees and volunteers. Ray keeps tabs on the grant and charitable giving."

"How about the rehab in Greensburg? You said it's a profit-making facility."

She took a sip of her tea and frowned. "Northerners don't know how to do tea." She emptied three packets of an artificial sweetener into her glass and stirred. "There's a director for that center as well. It's a little different since they have more employees and ones that are trained in their fields. Less volunteers. They have a small accounting office, but I get their financial statements. Ray expects them to make him a profit."

"Does that profit subsidize the other two centers?"

"Oh no. It subsidizes Ray Brockman."

Interesting.

~*~

We stepped inside the Botanical Gardens at Phipps, moving from autumn to a balmy summer atmosphere. It welcomed us with a splash of color and fragrance. I found myself with a different Caroline—one I liked much better.

"Oh look. A gardenia. Breathe in and imagine a backyard filled with that aroma." She lowered her eyes and inhaled the sweetness. "Oh, and there's redbud and crepe myrtles. We have all of them around our house. It's incredible when they're all in bloom." She became a portrait of excitement. Yet with each discovery, a shadow crossed her face.

"When's the last time you were home?"

She stood, pulling her face from the hibiscus. Her snarky side resurfaced with speed. "Are you writing my exposé?"

"Just wondering. You seem to be missing it."

"I haven't been home since I left two years ago. Seems I'm no longer welcomed there. My good southern family didn't approve of my new relationship. No more questions, Mr. Reporter."

"Sorry. No more questions." I put my arm around her shoulder to provide some element of comfort.

She stared at me, raised her eyebrows in question, and walked away, finding another hibiscus to smell.

~*~

Today had been quite amusing, but I needed to get back to business. I had Tyler to worry about, needed to get notes on paper, and I still needed a third contact.

I opened the door to find Tyler and Stella on opposite sides of the Scrabble board, Ginger laying on the floor, and takeout containers from the café beside them.

"So, the tour guide returns. Phipps ready to hire you?" Stella's eyes never left the game board as she spoke.

I kicked off my shoes. "They can't afford me. Who's winning?"

"The kid's killing me."

That brought the first full smile I'd seen on Tyler's face. "I read a lot. Helps with the vocabulary."

"Well I cook a lot, and I'm saying uncle. Got things to do at the deli."

I walked outside to have a word with Stella. She made no eye contact with me, and I wasn't sure why.

"You OK, Stel?"

She swung around to face me. "Why wouldn't I be?"

"I don't know. You seem kind of hurried. Are you upset I brought Tyler here?"

That softened her face to its normal pleasantness. She pointed toward the house. "That's a nice young man. I hate to say you were right, but...guess you were right."

"I hoped you'd see it, too. I want you to know he was leaving that business even before I caught up with him. He almost hopped on a bus to leave town before I located him. He knows right from wrong. He needs to catch a break here."

Stella reached one arm up to hug me. "Glad he found you."

Her hug lingered a little longer than usual, convincing me that something still troubled her.

"Stel, you sure you're OK?"

"Yep. I'm fine. Did you have an enjoyable time today?"

"Sure. Phipps is a beautiful facility."

"And your date? Did she enjoy it?" She emphasized the word *date*.

"She did. Not exactly a date. More of a business investment."

She arched one eye. "Hmph. What was she wearing?"

I leaned back and squinted at her. Where had that question come from?

"Skirt and sweater. Why?"

"Short skirt and heels?"

"I guess short, and yes, heels."

She nodded. "It was a date. Gotta go. Call me when you get hungry."

She walked the distance to her house without looking back. I watched until she entered and shook my head. What had gotten into her?

Tyler had already put away the Scrabble and tossed the food containers into the trash.

"Hope that was OK. She stopped with lunch for us, and when I told her you had a date, she stayed and ate with me."

"Always OK. She's a good neighbor."

He paused as he wiped the table and turned,

regarding me. "That all she is?"

"What does that mean?"

"I thought it may be something more."

I shook my head. "No, not with Stella. She's a good friend."

"Does she see it that way?"

"Of course. We've always been friends." Where did that come from? "Hey, let me show you what I'm working on."

I opened my laptop and clicked on my notes for Pete.

"The highlights indicate missing facts I'm still working to track down."

Peter (need last name), born in Somerset County in 1950

Youngest of six siblings

Married, (need date, wife's name, children)

Served in the United States Marines, part of the Wild Weasels, POW for two years

Returned with signs of PTSD and began drinking

Worked on construction site, welder, and truck driver at various times

Alcohol interfered with each employment

Wife died in (need year)

Tried rehab (need dates)

Became homeless at the age of (???)"

Tyler scanned the printed notes as I read aloud.

"Well, I'm no reporter, and I've never met this guy, but I could've written that. That fits half the men on the streets."

A defensive tension gripped my chest. It was preliminary. I had a vision for how it would come together.

"It's not done. These are notes. It doesn't have any

resemblance to what I'll write. It's the way I put it together that will give him some identity, some..." I searched for a word. "Some humanity."

"So what are you going to do with me? I still haven't decided to let you use my name."

How could I convince Tyler that my words would represent him well? Without a real name and pictures, the story would lose significant impact.

"Ty, you've been a victim all your life. I want to show that you've risen above all of the junk that life has thrown at you, and you've come out on top."

"Well, you might be a long time waiting. I'm not on top of anything yet." A little grin came. "Except the Scrabble game."

I gave his shoulder a playful punch. "You will be."

"If I climb out of the pit, will I want to be looking back down into it? And have the world read about the worst part of my life?"

"Ty, trust me on this. I think you'll be happy with the end result. Hey, I'm headed to town tonight. You want to come and meet Pete and D.J?"

He shook his head. "If it's all the same to you, I'd like to stay as far away from town as possible."

"Oh yeah. Forgot." I glanced at Ginger curled up and pressing against Ty's leg while she slept. "Well, I guess Ginger can stay at home. She likes your company. Did you find something to read?"

"Yeah, I took a few books to my room. Is that OK?"

I glanced to see the one sitting on the end table. "Integrity in Journalism."

Why, Tyler?

16

Claire Bassett

It didn't take long before Jonathan was asking me out again.

"Saturday afternoon. How about that Lake Arthur picnic? We're running out of days before the snow flies."

I shook my head. "I can't. I need to save weekend days for Isabella. She's in school all week and needs time with me."

"Bring her. I'd love to meet her. You know how smitten I am with Hannah."

That would definitely not happen. I gave him a sad smile. "You know I can't do that."

"OK. Saturday night? How about a movie?"

"Not this Saturday. I've got some things I need to do."

Things like reading my daughter a book or watching a movie with my parents.

I couldn't fully explain. I did want to see him again, but every weekend felt like a commitment I wasn't prepared to make. My mother would jump to conclusions. She'd have me out looking for a divorce lawyer. Besides all of that, I was far too vulnerable around him. No, I needed to limit the time spent with

Jonathan.

I offered an alternative so he wouldn't be too disheartened. "How about the following Saturday? A movie sounds good. I haven't been to one for ages."

He flashed a broad grin. "The following Saturday it is. I'll check to see what's playing when it gets closer."

"I better get back to work." I swept my hand over the stacks of paper on my desk. This was our workplace, deserving of respect. There were enough wagging tongues whispering my name.

"Lunch today?"

Without answering, I repeated my hand motion, indicating a heavy work load.

With his back to anyone within view, he touched his fingers to his lips, and with the same fingers, tapped my cheek. Then he turned and was gone. My cheek warmed with the heat of his touch.

~*~

I was two separate people with two distinct focuses. I continued to pray for Andrew, to caress the face in my frame, and dampen my pillow at night with tears. And then I'd find myself eager to walk into my office, see Jonathan's impish grin, and feel him weaving his fingers with mine. How double-minded was that. I was betraying both men.

And if that wasn't enough confusion for my mind, I kept seeing Andrew sleeping in doorways or begging for food. That seed of thought was planted even though my logical mind told me it was impossible. Every time it surfaced, I chased it away with a prayer or Bible verse or by humming a tune. Anything to erase the picture. *Take captive every thought.*

Following dinner, Dad took Isabella and Drew for a short walk around the neighborhood. A text message came in, but I continued cleaning the dishes.

Mother turned toward the sound. "Claire, did I hear your phone making little noises?"

I dried a plate and stacked it with the others. "Yes, Mom. No hurry. It's in my bedroom. I'll get it in a little bit."

She stopped in the middle of wiping Drew's highchair tray. "Do you want me to go get it for you?"

"No, thanks. I'm almost done here."

I so needed my own place. My parents meant well, they really did. I desperately needed their help. But the heart of me missed the control of my own home. Every day it was the same. I'd check my incoming text messages. She'd ask me who it was. I'd have to explain. It was probably one of the girls from the neighborhood checking on me. But it could be Jonathan, and then I'd have to dodge my mother's questions.

I hung the dishtowel up to dry, peeked in the yard, and saw that Dad was back with the kids. I pulled my bedroom door behind me. The message was from Molly. I saw the subject line before opening it. *This is the man Jason saw.*

As the attachment opened, a stranger, thin with shaggy clothing and a receding hairline appeared. As the pixels came together, there was the face of my husband. A gasp left my throat. Surely my mother would come running. My legs refused to hold me, and I collapsed onto the bed.

He was alive. Alive and living as if he had no

home, no family. What should I do? How would I find him? The playing field went from anywhere in the whole world to the streets of downtown Pittsburgh.

"Claire, are you coming out? Dad needs to leave for his church meeting."

"Coming." How could I go out and take care of my children when my life was toppling?

"Who was on the phone, Claire?"

It took her longer than usual. "It was Molly checking in on me."

"I'm glad you have such good friends."

~*~

Tomorrow was a work day. I desperately wanted to change my day from Wednesday to Thursday. I was told I could do that anytime I desired, but I couldn't fabricate a believable story for my parents. I certainly wasn't ready to tell them about this latest news.

When I got to my desk, once again my chair contained a surprise photo, a still life. It took me a moment to realize what it was. Dante's. The table we shared, or one like it, complete with a center candle, table setting, and a bottle of Merlot. It could be vintage Italy and would be beautiful framed. But today, I couldn't even muster a smile. I slid it into the drawer where I kept my purse and got busy with my tasks, thankful for a cubicle in the back of the room.

No one bothered me except to call out a "good morning," and I didn't venture away from my desk until lunchtime. I picked up my bagged lunch and disappeared into the confines of my car. I ate my sandwich while driving nowhere.

Riding on rural roads was the best I could do to avoid seeing people and holding casual conversations. Yet I couldn't hide from my own thoughts. I purposely turned my attention to the landscape, taking in details to occupy my mind.

The trees were almost bare, a few straggling leaves holding on even while their color faded to a lifeless brown. The occasional burst of color came from fall-blooming mums in orange, gold, and russet. As I turned back onto campus, green grass replaced the colors of autumn.

I parked and returned to the complex that housed my cubicle in the far corner. But my solitude had ended. Jonathan was loitering around the office, no doubt waiting for my return.

"Well, how'd you like it?" he asked the moment I sat down.

"The picture? It was beautiful. Thank you." I took a deep breath. "Jonathan, I have tons to do today, and I'm a little distracted. I need some space."

He held his hands up in submission. "Space you will have. I'll talk with you later in the week." If his feelings were hurt, he didn't show it.

Before returning to my tasks, I opened a search engine and began to hunt for anything about the homeless in Pittsburgh. A few resources came up, and I intended to visit each. I'd print the picture and show it in each place. Tomorrow—my day off. I couldn't take Drew, but I couldn't leave him home without providing explanations.

I picked up the phone. "Molly, will you watch Drew tomorrow? I'll explain when I get there."

"Of course I will. You OK?"

"No, not one little bit. Talk with you in the

morning." Far from OK, and I couldn't masquerade. I'd find an excuse to take the kids out somewhere this evening, or my parents would see right through to the heart of me. In the morning, I'd tell them that Drew and I would be visiting a friend.

17

Scott Harrington

October 19. Edwin's birthday. He should be turning thirty-five today. Nineteen years and still I hadn't done anything that measured up to all Edwin could have been. All that Charles Harrington wanted in a son. My father had been determined that a son of his would attend his alma mater. That dream died with Edwin.

I perused the awards on my shelf, the plaque on my wall. Paltry accomplishments. Edwin was on target to be valedictorian, headed to Yale. I'd never have gotten in even before I turned my back on law school.

All of a sudden, even the coveted Pulitzer seemed insignificant. Perhaps my real accomplishments wouldn't be quite so visible. Perhaps helping to stop a drug ring and getting a troubled kid off the streets would be enough. I didn't need external approval from those around me. I only needed it from two people. One would never give it. The other one was dead.

I'd work for the Pulitzer. When the project ended, I might check into a foreign correspondent position. I'd been approached about that in the past but hesitated to abandon visions of a normal life with a wife, kids, and a minivan. That started to feel like a pipedream. I chuckled. What man has a pipedream that included a minivan? I guess it wrapped into a bundle I called *normal*.

Back to my to-do list: find Sam Pulkowski; get missing info on Pete, including birth name, wife, children; consider D.J.; try to get him talking; stop to see Caroline. No, scratch that last item. She didn't fit into a bundle anywhere close to normal. Reporting in a foreign land would be more normal than Caroline McMann.

I donned my scrubby clothes, retrieved my backpack, and hopped on a bus into town. I'd get to the parking lot shed early and have Pete and D.J. talking before alcohol stole Pete's consciousness.

~*~

Once again, the lot attendant paid no attention as I went in. This time, I beat D.J. and Pete. Turning on my flashlight, I studied the dilapidated shed.

Everything lay stacked on top of other things with no semblance of order. An old file cabinet and desk served as the foundation, topped with orange traffic cones, metal chairs, and cardboard boxes wrinkled from the dampness. Bags of road salt appeared to be the only things that didn't belong in a dumpster. I now expected the scurrying of little feet near the back of the shed.

I retrieved my silenced phone from the zippered compartment of my backpack and snapped pictures, making sure I included Pete's sleeping mat and D.J.'s cardboard. I had my phone hidden before I heard them arrive.

"Well, lookie here. We got us an early visitor. Ain't

seen you for a few days."

"Hey, Pete. Yeah, I moved around a little bit. How you doing, D.J.?"

"Me and D.J., we've been doin' the same. Ain't we Deej?" Pete answered for him.

D.J. nodded without speaking. So much for getting him talking.

Pete eased himself down to his mat, holding tight to the bottle gripped in his hand. D.J. watched Pete, waiting for him to be down and settled before he moved to spread out his own things.

Pete sat on his mat with his back leaning against an oversized box, took a long drink, and let out a contented sigh.

"So, Pete, you said you grew up in Johnstown, PA. How'd you end up in Pittsburgh?"

"The Burgh," he said it with fondness. "Moved here before the war. That's where all the jobs was."

With a deep swig from his bottle, he held it out to share with me. I waved it away, and asked, "What job brought you here?"

A little chortle. "Well, truth be told, it was prob'ly more a lady than a job. But in them days, you needed a job to make the lady pay you any mind."

Keep him talking. "Yeah, I think most ladies like to see a paycheck these days, too. Who was the lady?"

His eyes sparkled with the memory. "Miss Jewel. Miss Jewel Weston," he whispered it like a prayer, shifted his eyes to the bottle, and took a long, slow drink.

D.J. glared at me.

"Did you get the girl? Marry her?" Jewel Weston. There had to be some info on her out there.

"Yep. We done got married a'for I headed out to

Nam."

"What's your game here?" D.J. stepped into the conversation. I'd wanted to get him talking, and now he was. He sat straight up, his eyes drilling me.

"What do you mean?"

"Just what I asked. What's your game? What're you doing here probing and questioning? You a cop? A reporter?"

"Hey, I'm here passing the time. I enjoy hearing about people." I turned his question back to him. "What's your game, D.J.? You're not the same as them. You always live here in the 'burgh?"

"Pass the time on someone else, and leave Pete be. He's more fragile than you think."

I glanced at Pete to see his reaction, but he had disappeared into the bottle.

I sat quiet for a moment. "Thanks for watching out for him. You're a good friend."

"Just leave him be." With that, D.J. aimed his flashlight at his Bible and read.

Pete finished the bottle and soon passed out. Then I lay down, remembering Edwin when we were still young and best friends. Friends take care of each other. Only, I didn't take care of him.

Sometime later, when I began to drift off, strange, raspy breaths brought me back again.

D.J. jumped up and began shaking Pete. "Pete! You OK? Sit up."

He propped him into a sitting position, but Pete fought for air. He wheezed as he attempted to fill his lungs, eyes growing wide with panic.

He turned toward me. "Get the attendant. Have somebody call 9-1-1."

I stood up to yell for someone outside, but the lot

had emptied, no sign of anyone in the darkness of night.

I did the quickest thing I could—grabbed my silenced cell phone from the bottom of my backpack, dialed 9-1-1, and gave them our location. Even in his state of anxiety, D.J. shot me a knowing look.

Emergency services are efficient in the city, and an ambulance blared its way into the parking lot in minutes. We waited with the door opened. Pete's pasty, gray pallor made his expressionless eyes appear huge. The paramedics started oxygen and loaded him into the ambulance. D.J. climbed in with him.

"Which hospital? I'll meet you there."

"Allegheny General." And they sped off, leaving me alone in the parking lot. I didn't look forward to the walk across town and over the bridge in the middle of the night, but buses wouldn't be running. I took a last gaze around to make sure no live ashes from Pete's last cigarette remained. I spotted D.J.'s discarded Bible and his backpack. I would take them to him, along with Pete's grocery bag and panhandling signs.

As I opened the backpack to drop the Bible inside, I saw a wallet. Why does a poor man who won't panhandle need a wallet? I couldn't resist looking inside. It was empty of any money, not a dollar, not a coin. But it held a driver's license with the name Andrew Bassett.

His photo ID showed a cleaned up and younger version of the man, the date two years earlier. That would make him thirty-nine, about six years older than me.

A business card behind the driver's license said *Chaulders and Associates, Andrew Bassett, Senior Accounting Manager*. Accounting?

"I play the numbers," he told me. Is this what he meant? Or did he gamble? Embezzle? What would bring him down this low?

As I returned the wallet to the backpack, I spotted an envelope. It wasn't sealed, and the flap showed the wear and tear of frequent use. There were pictures inside. A newborn baby with a blue blanket and knitted hat. A little girl with a mass of spiral curls and an impish smile. A professional photo of him, a lady, and the little girl. It would take something significant to make him leave this family. Or had they left him? I remembered his fixation on the little girl that passed on the city street. She also had curls. Had he been thinking of his daughter?

I took out my notebook and wrote as much as I could. I slid each picture from the envelope and read the back. The names Andrew, Claire, and Isabella were etched on the reverse of the family picture. Someone had printed *Isabella Bassett* on the girl's picture and *Drew James Bassett* on the baby. Andrew—D.J.—Drew James.

This was my third bio. I would write the story about Andrew Bassett—D.J. But first, I'd make my way to the hospital to check on Pete.

~*~

I trekked across the Rachel Carson Bridge toward Allegheny General Hospital. Still shivering from my night walk, I passed through hospital security to enter the emergency room. D.J. sat hunched-over in the waiting area, head down and hands folded. Unsure if he was praying or deep in thought, I waited a few moments before placing my hand on his shoulder. He startled, his head jolting up.

"How's he doing? Any word?"

He shook his head. "No. Nothing much. They told me they stabilized him, but he needs some tests."

"Pete'll hate that."

D.J. offered a slight grin. "He sure will. And all without his bottle." He ran his hands through his hair before speaking again. "I think he has emphysema, or lung cancer, or something like that. It's getting worse."

"Is there anyone we can call? Any family?"

D.J. was quiet for a moment, probably deciding how much to tell. "There's a daughter. Mary Anne. I don't know her married name. Maiden name is Simmons. Last Pete knew, she lived in Monroeville."

I sat across from him. "Does he ever see her? Talk with her? Does she know about him?"

D.J. shook his head. "He doesn't want her to know how he's living. He's convinced she wouldn't forgive him for the years of alcohol. Her mother died while he binged. Department of Social Services put her in the foster system when she was fifteen. He tried to clean up so he could get her, but he couldn't do it."

I had learned more about Pete in these last two minutes than in all the time I spent fishing for information.

"So what are you going to do now? Oh, by the way, here's your pack. Do you want to keep Pete's with you?"

For all of D.J.'s mistrust of me, he didn't question whether I looked at anything inside.

"I'll take the backpacks. I'll hang out here 'til morning and see what I can find out."

I leaned forward, elbows on my knees. "What can

I do?"

He assessed me for a long minute. "What exactly do you do?"

I almost told him, but we were both too weary.

"That's a story for another day. Know this—I won't do anything to hurt him. Or you either. Buses should start running in about a half an hour. I'll head on out of here and be back tomorrow to see what the doctors say. Can I bring anything for you?"

"You can bring some answers."

I reached in my wallet and pulled out a twenty.

"I don't need that."

"There's no free breakfast here. Please take it."

D.J. rubbed the weariness from his eyes, his shoulders slumped. I laid the money on the backpack that had been placed in the chair beside his.

"Tomorrow, come with some answers."

18

Scott Harrington

Tyler always had a book in his hand. It took me a few minutes to realize what he was reading. As he turned a page, I saw pictures of the Cathedral of Learning, the gothic architecture of the University of Pittsburgh.

"Pretty remarkable architecture, isn't it?"

He looked up from the book. "Yeah, it is." A shadow crossed his face, and he returned to reading.

"You ever been inside the cathedral?"

He scowled. "Only in books."

I pulled up a chair and sat down. "What's going on, Tyler? What are you thinking?"

He closed the book and looked up. "Sorry. Just daydreaming. College was never an option for me. I need some kind of trajectory in my life. Something beyond living day to day."

"There's nothing wrong with daydreaming. Everyone needs to have goals, something to reach for. Have you thought about yours? What would you like to see happen in your life?"

He sat pensively, slow to answer. "It's funny how goals are rooted in a person's circumstances. My goal had been to get a job, any job that would get me back to my old rented room. At the time, it was a desperate goal. But now, staying here with you, in a nice quiet neighborhood away from the city, I feel like my goals are changing."

"That's not a bad thing."

He released a sarcastic laugh. "Maybe not. But nothing's really changed from when I lived on the street. I still have no family, no job, and no possibility for college. I can't keep imposing on you."

"You're not imposing, Ty. Kids your age are supposed to be dependent on someone. Here's a little piece of advice for whatever it's worth. You can set a goal, but unless you back it with a plan, it's only a pipedream. Think about what you want, and let's see if we can work out a plan."

Tyler pulled a folded paper from his pocket and scanned it before handing it to me. I took the creased page and read it. *Ty, I'm leaving to make a better life for us. I need a little time to get settled and I'll come get you. Hang in there, buddy. Love you. Dad.*

I refolded it and handed it back. "You kept this all these years?"

He shifted to return the page to his pocket. "Yeah, but I don't know why. My mom and dad, they worried about themselves and had nothing left over for their son. Not enough money, not enough time, not enough love. The note's just a lie in writing. I'm sure he made a better life, one that didn't have the responsibilities of a son."

Something about Tyler's dad nagged at me. The pieces didn't seem to fit. A father who took his kid fishing and to baseball games. The note saying he'd come back to get him. I couldn't quite buy into the theory that he'd managed to forget about him.

"So let's get back to the goal. What do you want to

do with your life? Don't think about the obstacles."

Tyler managed a small smile. "I guess I want what you have. A small house in a nice neighborhood. A job where I can feel like I'm doing something important."

I needed to let that sink in. Tyler wanted what I had. Yet it didn't satisfy me. I wanted more. Another award to hang with the others. "Let's get past this police investigation. While we're waiting, you have plenty of time to start some inquiries. Do some checking on financial aid and scholarships. Then we'll put plans to that goal." I stood and pushed my chair back. "I'm headed into town to see Pete. Sorry to leave you alone."

"No problem. I think I'll walk down to the café and say hi to Stella. Now that's a lady that will make a good mother someday. I need to add that to my goal. Marry someone just like Stella."

19

Claire Bassett

We sat at Molly's kitchen table. I could see out her French doors to where my rockers sat in her sunroom. She had placed a rose-patterned cushion on the seats and had a knitted throw over the back of one.

"Molly, why didn't Jason go over to him? Talk or try to help? Why didn't he bring him home?"

She leaned forward and took my hands. "Honey, Andrew's an adult. He isn't there because he has nowhere to go. He's there because he needed to get away. To think things through. Don't you think he would have been humiliated if Jason had approached him?"

My shoulders tensed and I lifted my chin. "I'm not worried about his humiliation. I'm worried about getting him home."

Molly met my sharp tone with her calming words. "We will. And we'll get him help."

We were silent for a moment. I reached over to hug her. "I have to go. Thanks for keeping Drew."

Molly walked me to the door. "Claire, go easy on yourself. It's a big city."

~*~

My list had three names of agencies that provided resources for the homeless—Hope House, Three Rivers Missions, and LifeWay. I would start with Hope House. I had my phone picture, but I also printed it in a 5x7 photo. I would show it to everyone I could, hoping for any kind of lead.

I hated city driving, especially during the busy rush hour. I wound around the spiral path of the parking garage until I found an empty space on the third level. My destinations were spread out, but I'd leave my car and walk. If necessary, I'd hop on a bus for a few blocks.

I started with Hope House and got nowhere. The office was tucked between a diner and a cigar shop, only a doorway with lettering.

Inside, a receptionist greeted me.

"I'm hoping you can help me." I pulled out the flyer and turned it toward her. "I'm looking for this man."

She took it and examined it. "No. This is not one of our residents. He's never been here." She handed it back to me.

"Can you be sure? Do you know them all?"

She leaned back in her chair and nodded. "I know them all. He's not here."

"Do you think any of your residents will recognize him? Could I go in and show the picture around?"

She shook her head. "No, ma'am. We protect the identity of our residents." Then she stood, obviously indicating the end of our meeting.

Three Rivers Mission was five blocks away. Thankful I wore my athletic shoes, I made my way there, only to discover the door locked and a sign indicating it would open at five o'clock, seven hours from now. An alley beside it offered a side door. I knocked. No one answered. Three Rivers Mission would have to wait for another day.

LifeWay had a small office, not an open environment where homeless people came. Two women and one man worked in the close quarters. They shook their heads when I showed the picture.

"We don't work directly with the men. We work behind the scenes, raising money for healthcare and food lines. We support the people who work with them."

My shoulders slumped, and I breathed a heavy sigh. Three closed doors.

"Do you have any suggestions for me?"

Their suggestions were already on my list—Hope House and Three Rivers Mission. I thanked them and walked back outside.

My next step would be labor intensive. I began canvasing the city, going to panhandlers and anyone that looked like they might be in that culture. Three hours later, aching and exhausted, I was no closer to finding Andrew.

My throbbing feet carried me back to the parking garage and up to level three. I unlocked my car and sat with my head resting against the steering wheel. What now? I pulled my phone out of my handbag and called off work tomorrow.

Back in the northern suburbs, I turned into my neighbor's driveway, glancing over to my own home. With leaden legs, I walked to Molly's front door. I wanted to be in my house across the street, gardening, cooking, and waiting for Andrew to return from work.

I tucked Drew in his car seat, my movements slow

and sluggish. Molly stood at her driveway with her arms crossed and her brows furrowed.

"I'm worried about you, Claire. Are you all right to drive?"

"I have to be all right. I have no other choice." My voice went flat. I had no energy for talking. "I called off work, but I'm going to leave Drew with my parents. I'll leave the same time as I do every morning, and they'll think I'm working."

"OK. I'm getting a sitter and coming with you. Give me the photo, and I'll get duplicates made."

"You don't have to do that. It's not a pleasant task."

"No arguments, my friend. We can cover twice as much territory. What time will you pick me up?"

~*~

Mom and Isabella were setting the table when I got home. Drew slept in my arms.

"Oh my," my mother exclaimed. "This is way too late for his nap. That baby won't sleep tonight."

"He played himself out. I'm going to let him sleep."

"But, Claire…"

"Mom, it's fine." My voice did nothing to hide my annoyance. She stiffened and returned to placing each piece of silverware on a perfectly folded napkin.

"Sorry, Mom. It's been a long day."

No response followed. Now that I'd offended her, I couldn't ask her to watch the kids. I'd have to take them with me and leave them with one of the neighbors. That meant leaving the city, driving forty-five minutes home and timing it so it would match my work routine, picking up the kids, driving back to Molly's, and returning to the city. Did I have the energy for that? I didn't, but that couldn't deter me. I had to be at Three Rivers Mission for their five o'clock opening.

~*~

The next morning, my mother appeared to have forgotten my offensive retort or perhaps forgiven me. Before leaving for what she thought was work, I asked her if she would mind if I met some friends for dinner and came home late.

Her eyes lit up as she said, "Certainly, dear. Have a nice time."

Let her assume I would meet Jonathan. It made my day a whole lot easier.

I pulled my car into Molly's driveway at eight thirty as planned, my eyes avoiding the other side of the street. This morning I couldn't bear to see someone else living in my home. When she didn't come right out, I went to the door. Jan opened it, and I heard voices from the kitchen.

"Come on in. We have a slight change in plans."

Inside, I found Molly, Jan, and Rebecca setting a table with quiche, fresh fruit salad, and muffins.

"Can't start out without a little energy. We're going to enjoy some breakfast, and then we're all going to town." The aroma of coffee filled the room. Fresh blackberries, strawberries, and kiwi topped the salad. A bowl filled with floating candles and fall blossoms were placed in the center. It presented like a table my mother would set, prim and proper with a little flair. Tears sprung to my eyes.

"Thank you," I whispered.

Rebecca stepped up to hug me. "We'll find him. Don't worry. He's never been a match against all of us. When we gang up, he knows we'll win."

Despite the party atmosphere, it was a somber day. We finished eating and loaded into Jan's SUV. We planned to go out two by two, starting with Molly and me, Jan and Rebecca. Streets were divided up by geography. We would meet at noon at The Point to compare notes. We all had cell phones in case by some miracle, we spotted Andrew.

For the second day in a row, my feet ached and my spirit sank.

"No one knows him. The photo is current, the way he looks now, not with him cleaned up and dressed in business clothes. And in the same corner where Jason saw him. What do I do now?"

Molly draped her arm across my slumped shoulders. "Stand firm, Claire. Jason saw him twice. He'll appear again.

Jan and Rebecca hurried across the intersection before the light changed back to red. Jan waved her notebook for us to see.

"We got a lead," she called from a distance. When they got close enough, she opened the notebook.

"Two people recognized him. One guy who looked like a businessman of some sort, said he had seen him a few times, always with an older man, but couldn't remember an exact location. But here's the big one."

She motioned to Rebecca to share. "We talked to a man who looked more like a street person. He told us that he saw him at breakfast many times at St. John's Episcopal Church. We went over to the church and talked with a few people. Seems the City Outreach serves breakfast there every weekday beginning at six o'clock."

This was Friday. Monday was a workday. Could I arrange something for Monday? I'd already called off today and couldn't mess up this job.

Andrew had been gone a year. It would have to wait one more day.

20

Scott Harrington

I parked near the ER entrance and walked past the crowded waiting room. I didn't see D.J. in the waiting area, so I made my way to find Pete.

Pete was no longer in ICU. They'd moved him into his own room. D.J. sat in a chair near the window, a curtain separating Pete from the empty bed in the front of the room. I walked in, peeking around the curtain to see Pete, the head of his bed with a slight incline. The oxygen mask dangled from the clear tubing beside the bed.

"Well how-de-do there, Scotty." Pete's thundering voice had become a raspy whisper. With a feeble effort, he lifted his hand to mine. I took it for the briefest moment.

"You're looking good today. Lots better than the last time I saw you."

"And feelin' better, too. That there young doc is comin' in to sign me out any time now."

"We don't know that, Pete," D.J. spoke up. "The nurse said he's coming in to talk, not to sign you out."

"Well there ain't no reason to keep a man a'layin' in bed when he's done got hisself better."

"Let's hear him out. You're feeling better because

they have all this medicine flowing through you." D.J. pointed toward the IV line.

"That? It's some water to keep me peeing. I don't know why they's always wantin' to save that stuff."

I shook my head and stifled a laugh. What a character. Never wanting for more than he had. We could all learn from Old Pete.

He launched into one of his coughing spells, causing the nurse to hurry into the room. He waved her off as he had done with me on occasion. She paid him no mind, and with skilled hands, covered the lower half of his face with the oxygen mask.

When his coughing stopped, she prepared an injection for his IV. Looking at his hospital wristband, she asked, "Name and date of birth?"

"Yinz done asked me that already."

"And we'll be asking you again and again. You wouldn't want me to be giving you the wrong meds, would you?"

"No, ma'am. I'm Pete Simmons, born in 1947."

"Good. When's your birthday, Pete?"

He sighed, demonstrating his boredom with the question. "August 25th. Same as I told yinz before."

Pete tugged at the mask.

The nurse playfully swatted his hand. "You leave that be. Doctor will be here in a minute, and he better see you with oxygen."

With that, she emptied the syringe into his IV line.

"Deej, I done told 'em you's my kin," Pete mumbled through the mask. "Don't say ya ain't, or they might not let me outta here." As if in a flash of inspiration, he turned toward me.

"Scotty, you can be my kin, too. I got me two sons. Ain't that sumpin'?"

When the doctor arrived, he shook hands with D.J. and then me and asked, "Are you family?"

Pete answered for us.

"Yep, they's my kin, all the kin I got."

The doctor cocked his head and gave Pete a knowing gaze. "OK." He pulled up a chair and indicated we might want to do the same. Opening his laptop, he made a few clicks. "Pete, you had a serious attack on your lungs."

"Sure did, Doc. And look how quick yinz got me feelin' better." He pulled off the mask. "That daggone nurse was a'thinkin' I needed this thing."

The corner of the doctor's mouth rose. "Well you can keep it off for now, but remember, that nurse is part of the reason you're feeling better."

"Oh, yesirree. I ain't meanin' no disrespect."

"Pete, you have lung cancer. I'm sorry to have to bring you this news. Your cancer appears to be in an advanced stage. We're waiting for the full biopsy report to identify the exact type and stage, but a team of physicians concur and are confident that it's non-small cell lung cancer in stage four. That's the most common type. We know both lungs are impacted, as well as the tissues surrounding the lungs. More testing would show us if other organs have been affected."

He paused to let us absorb that news. "I'm going to give you some options for treatment and our recommendations. A hospital social worker will be joining us to provide some options for non-medical arrangements."

"Slow down there, Doc. Yinz ain't a'plannin' none of that chemo-type stuff, are you?"

"It's a big part of the treatment plan, Pete. We would like to start with radiation to shrink the tumors and follow with a series of sequential chemotherapy treatments."

"No, siree. I ain't a'gettin' that stuff. Saw what it did to my wife and didn't help her anyways. No, sir. I'll be a'gettin' goin when you sign them there papers."

"You mentioned the social worker," D.J. said to the doctor. "Obviously, Pete can't pay for his care. Are there some options for help? Assisted living? Rehab? Anything that addresses needs of those in the poverty range?"

The doctor turned his attention toward D.J. and nodded. "There are, and I'll let her give you all of that information. I know Pete is without a home, and I know he has an alcohol addiction. We saw signs of withdrawal and have kept him well sedated, but those signs are going to resurface. A rehab facility is the best option to deal with that."

The doctor's fingers flew over the keyboard, logging anything pertinent from this conversation.

"Now just you two be a'waitin'. Don't be makin' plans to put me somewhere. I got me a home, and I'm heading on down there today. I got all I'll be needin'."

The doctor turned toward him. "Pete, does that home have heat? It's October, almost November. An unheated building will accelerate your condition and you'll be right back here."

"You ain't givin' me none of that chemo stuff." With his bottom lip jutted out, head tilted downward, he looked like a sulking child.

"Doctor, what's the outlook for Pete if he does follow your suggested treatment plan? Would it make a difference?" D.J. ignored Pete's outburst.

"It would shrink the tumors and provide his lungs with a little more breathing capacity. At this stage, the condition is terminal. It's a matter of when. Some people choose to be treated and have as long as we can give them. Pete's not the first to say no. It's a harsh treatment."

"See, I done told you that stuff ain't no good." Pete jumped in.

"How long?" D.J. asked, ignoring Pete.

"Only God knows that answer, but from my experience, with treatment, three to six months. Without treatment and maintaining his current lifestyle, I wouldn't expect two weeks."

"What if he had no treatment, but a better living arrangement, like a rehab or comfortable home?"

"We have drugs that can help the breathing but won't deal with the cancer. It will grow and take his life. But with a better home situation and pharmacological help, I'd guess two months. We can never say for sure."

D.J. turned to Pete. "Pete, you're not leaving today. We need to find a better place for you."

"You put me in one of them there nursing home places, and I'll be a'walkin' out. And I ain't doing no chemo."

"No chemo. But we need to talk about finding you someplace warmer."

"We can keep him here for another day or two to better stabilize him, but that's all I can do," the doctor addressed D.J. once again. "Without a treatment plan in place, I have to release him. We can't serve as a care facility."

"I understand. I'll have a solution in two days' time. What about the withdrawal?"

"He'll have signs, but we'll treat as best we can. We can reduce symptoms but can't eliminate them."

The doctor shook hands with D.J. and me, gave Pete a pat on the shoulder, and left us to wait for the social worker. Pete pouted like an angry child, his voice gaining strength.

"I never thought I'd see the day when my own kin would be a'turnin' on me."

I laughed. "We're not your kin, Pete."

"You sure ain't, and yinz ain't a'getting' nothing in my will."

We all laughed at that, even Pete. When he drifted off to sleep, we stepped outside the room.

"What are you thinking, D.J.?"

"I need to try to find his daughter. That's the only possibility besides a facility. I'm not sure where to start."

"Let me do the footwork there. I've got some connections." That reminded both of us that today I would be bringing D.J. some answers. But with perfect timing, the social worker showed up.

I offered to do what I do best. "Hey, I'll get working on finding Mary Anne. You can gather some info here."

"Mary Anne Simmons, maiden name. Last known address was Monroeville."

"If I find her, do you want me to make contact?"

"Yeah, I'll have my hands full keeping the old man in bed."

I headed to the parking garage, trying to determine the best way to start. Government offices would be closed for the weekend. I would have to do an Internet search. I retrieved my car and headed toward home. With limited time, I needed to avoid any distractions.

An hour later, I suggested Tyler take Ginger for a

walk, and then I sat at my computer. I turned my phone off since neither D.J. nor the hospital had my number anyway. It didn't take long to find her. Vital records, genealogy sites, and white pages all provided some leads. Three Mary Anne Simmons had been born in and around Pittsburgh in the past fifty years. Vital records showed which one had been born to Jewel and Peter Simmons. She later married and became Mary Anne Williams, divorced, and remarried a man with the last name of Marshall.

I debated calling or just showing up. I decided on the phone call but received an out-of-service message. Probably disconnected the landline.

There was no other choice then. I hopped in the car and set out to find the daughter of old Pete Simmons.

The GPS took me to a subdivision east of Pittsburgh. Most of the houses were modest brick ranch homes with some mature foliage. Not high end, but well kept. The house that I hoped still belonged to Mary Anne had a play gym inside a fenced yard. The lone swing set held a toddler seat with a small plastic slide beside it. Other toys lay scattered in the grass. Pete may be a grandpa. What would he say about that?

I rang the bell and a pregnant lady, much too young to be Pete's daughter, opened the door.

"Hi, I'm looking for Mary Anne Marshall. Is this the right home?"

"Yeah." She turned her head and called, "Mom, a man here to see you."

Mary Anne came to the door, drying her hands on a dishtowel. She wore the fatigued look of one whose life hadn't been easy. Her eyes appeared tired but soft. Maybe the heaviness of life hadn't calloused her spirit.

"I'm Mary Anne Marshall. How can I help you?"

"My name is Scott Harrington. Can I talk with you about your father?"

She took a step back and her eyes narrowed. "You're at the wrong house. I don't have a father."

She started to close the door, but I didn't back up.

"Pete Simmons? Is he your father?"

She turned and checked for her daughter, tossed the dishtowel on a chair, and stepped out onto the porch. She clicked the door behind her and crossed her arms over her chest.

"Peter Simmons is my father. I haven't seen him in years. I don't know where he is or if he's even still alive."

"He's alive. He's in Allegheny General. He's ill."

She sat on the porch swing and indicated I should sit in the chair facing her.

"What's wrong with him, cirrhosis of the liver?" The sarcasm hung heavy.

"No. Lung cancer. Stage four."

The swing rocked back and forth. She lowered her head and then lifted her gaze to me.

"Mr. Harrington, I can't help you. I'm sorry he's sick, but Pete Simmons is a stranger to me. No, let me restate that. He's not a stranger. He's the man who was out drinking every night after my mother, his wife, had chemo. I was fifteen. I'd hold her head over the toilet while she vomited from the treatments, trying to keep her pain at bay without giving her too much of her medication. Sometime after that, he would stagger in too drunk to walk straight. On a good night, he'd pass out. On a bad night, I'd be cleaning up after him. Fifteen years old."

For once, I had no words. "I'm so sorry."

"He was drunk when she died, drunk at the funeral, and drunk when DSS came and removed me from the home. No, I can't help you, and I don't want to see him."

I leaned forward, elbows on my knees. "I'm not going to tell you he's stopped drinking. He hasn't. But I will tell you he's not an ugly drunk, no meanness in him. He's happy most of the time. Doesn't ask for anything. He seems contented with what he has."

"And what exactly is that? Where does he live? How does he work?"

She didn't know.

"He's homeless. He lives on the streets in Pittsburgh, sleeps in a vacant shed. Panhandles for a little cash."

She shook her head back and forth. "Unbelievable. What do you want from me? What are you hoping will happen here?"

"Pete's terminal. If he had a place to live, he might have around two months left. If he goes back to the cold shed, it's doubtful he'll last a week. I hoped he could die with a little dignity in a home with family."

I asked the impossible, but it had to be asked. To her credit, she took some time before answering. No flat-out rejection. She sat staring at the porch floor, the swing stilled by her feet.

"Mr. Harrington—"

"Scott," I corrected.

Her softness returned but merged with a sadness. "Scott, I know this is going to make me sound like a terrible person, but I can't. My daughter is about to give birth, I have a toddler to watch, my husband travels for his business. I don't have the space or emotional energy to have my father come here."

"I understand." I nodded and then stood to leave. "Thank you for giving me some time, and I'm sorry I opened old wounds."

Mary Anne stood as well. "Does he have anyplace else to go?"

"We're talking with social services to see if there's a facility that will take him."

"Thank you for helping him. If it's not too much to ask, could someone let me know where he goes and when he...when he passes?"

"We can do that. Here's my card if you want to contact me."

"Thank you."

With that, I stepped from her porch and walked to my car. Mary Anne watched until I had pulled away. I regretted that there wouldn't be reconciliation, but I couldn't fault her. So what now?

21

Claire Bassett

"Claire, what in the world are you doing?" My mother stood there staring at me.

"I'm packing Bella's lunch. Why?" It should have been obvious.

"You've been standing there with that knife in your hand for five minutes not doing anything."

Had I done that? Distraction had been my constant companion while I attempted to perform everyday tasks. My hands and feet moved at my command, but my mind stayed focused on the city.

I set down the knife. "Oh, thinking about today. Lots to do at work."

"Well here, I'll finish that. You go get dressed."

I allowed her to take over, too weary to assert my independence this morning.

After a quick shower and sliding into the simplest, comfort clothing suitable for work, I managed to get Bella on the school bus and drove to the university under a gray October sky—a perfect match for me on this day. *Please let Jonathan be out today.* I couldn't handle any level of conversation with him.

But I didn't get my wish. After lunch, he strolled past the receptionist desk.

I glanced up to greet him without stopping my work. "Good morning, Jonathan."

"Don't you mean good afternoon? It's almost one."

My laugh came out as hollow as a drum. "Guess the day's going fast."

"Missed you Friday. Were you sick?"

"I didn't feel well." That was the truth.

"Better today?"

"A little," I lied. Maybe the stilted conversation would deter him?

No, he began to sit.

I stopped him with a shake of my head. "I have Friday's work to catch up on. Can we talk later?"

His disappointment showed, but he acted with kindness, as always. "I'll leave you to your work. Looking forward to Saturday."

Saturday. I had forgotten I'd agreed to an evening with him. Well, that was almost a week away and a lot could happen.

When I arrived home, I had to again explain that I would be gone tomorrow. I would take Drew to Molly's. Mom and Dad needed a break on my days off.

"Mom, I'll be going to Molly's tomorrow for a visit. We have breakfast planned, so I'm leaving early. I'm taking Drew. It's good for him to socialize with other kids."

She squinted. "You've been going there often."

"I know. You and Dad need some space, and I enjoy seeing my old friends."

She nodded her agreement but tilted her head in question. During dinner, she pried for information. "Is there anything new from the police? I haven't asked you for a while."

"I haven't heard from them and haven't tried to contact them. Guess I should do that while I'm in town."

"Anything new in your neighborhood? How are the renters?"

"They pay their rent. I don't know them, so I can't say how they are."

With a big sigh, she dropped the inquisition. No doubt it would resurface at some point. She had a keen instinct, and I was easy to read. I might tell them, depending on how tomorrow went.

~*~

The next morning, traffic along I-279 delayed my arrival at St. John's. It was six forty by the time I found a garage and made my way to the church. A chill in the air that would only get worse as winter approached, reminded me of the urgency to find Andrew and bring him home.

I tried the main door. Finding it locked, I set out walking to locate another doorway. A plain metal door off to the side posted a sign for the free breakfast hours.

I turned the knob and entered the large room, not sure what to expect. No one greeted me, and I saw no place to check in. The diners probably went up to the counter for their food. Although about twenty people were eating and four serving, the room felt empty because of its grand size.

Looking around, I shuddered at the defeated faces. The joyless meal served only enough sustenance to make it through another desolate day. Our mealtimes at home had been spent sharing anecdotes about our days, laughing at Bella's silliness. Our meals had been filled with bright eyes.

But my husband had chosen this place over his kitchen table—an old man his companion instead of his wife. I knew he suffered a deep grief, but why wasn't I enough?

After scanning the room for any sign of him, I moved from one table to the next, starting with the one seating the only other woman in the room. Her hair streaked with gray had been cut right at the base of her ears—a bowl cut. I suspected she chopped it herself. Grime embedded her mismatched clothing, and body odor hung heavily in the air. My heart broke for her, but I had to stay focused.

I sat across the white plastic table and spoke softly. "Good morning. I'm looking for someone and wondered if you might have seen him." I pulled out the picture of Andrew and laid it on the table in front of her. "I believe he comes here to eat breakfast."

She glanced at the picture, shook her head without ever looking up at me. When she opened her mouth to the fork filled with eggs, wide gaps were visible where teeth should be.

I moved to another table. A few people had seen Andrew, but no one knew him or where to find him. Each one said the same thing—that he came with an older man, and they ate breakfast here most every morning.

A man who had been serving behind the counter came out and sat down across from me.

"My name's Don. Can I help you with something? I see you taking a picture around to folks."

"Yes, I'm looking for this man. Do you know

him?"

He took my flyer and held it up. "Sure do. He's in here most every morning. Usually by now. I suspect he'll be in soon. You related to him?"

"He's my husband. He's sick and needs help."

"Well, he should be along soon. Didn't appear to be sick."

"I mean that he..." I couldn't finish. "Is it OK if I wait here?"

"Sure. Can I bring you something to eat?" His face displayed kindness.

"No, thank you. I'll wait over there." I motioned to a table off to the side and out of the way. I could see the door, but when Andrew walked in, he wouldn't see me.

People came and went. They ate their breakfast then took their lost dignity back to the streets.

Don returned to bring me coffee.

"Thought you might need this. Here's a little cream and sugar."

I thanked him as he left the tray for me.

By nine thirty, volunteers began cleaning the kitchen and locking the door. Andrew never arrived.

"Sorry, ma'am. Sure surprised he didn't show. You can try back any weekday."

"I can't come tomorrow, but I'll try Thursday." I felt a pulse in my throat and heard the crack in my voice. "If he comes, please don't tell him I'm looking for him."

"Sure thing." He gave an understanding nod and patted my shoulder.

I stood outside looking at the vastness before me. I didn't know where to go next. With heavy feet, I lumbered back to the parked car and headed for home.

22

Scott Harrington

After leaving Mary Anne, I debated going to the hospital or going home and decided to stop home first. I had no good news to share with D.J. or Pete. I needed Stella's ear. She had a knack for seeing things with clarity when I couldn't.

I stopped by the café, but they told me she wasn't in. Parking my car in my driveway, I walked next door, knocked and tried the door. It was locked. A key to her house was on my keyring, but I wouldn't use it while she was home.

She peeked out the window and opened the door. A glance told me that she had taken the day off. She wore jeans and a sweatshirt with her long hair loose.

Stella leaned back and held the door open wide. "You look terrible. What's going on?"

Leave it to Stella. She could read me like a book. I told her about Pete's cancer and about Mary Anne.

"I can't blame her. She's filled with bitterness. Plus, she has a lot going on in her own family. But Pete, he's such a likeable old guy. He'll be dead in a week if he goes back to the storage shed. I know what's going on in his head. If he's at a facility, he can't get a drink. His bourbon's more important than the time it would deny him."

"Obviously, the drinking isn't good for him, but what does it matter at this point. I say let the old guy have his bottle and be happy."

"I don't disagree, but I hate to see him lose the possibility of two more months, and I hate to see him die alone in that old outbuilding. It'll kill D.J. to watch him go."

Stella took my hand and wrapped her fingers through mine.

"Scott, I know what's on your mind, and I'll help you with whatever you decide."

I furrowed my brows. "How do you know what's on my mind when I don't know?"

She smiled. "You know."

I leaned back on her sofa and stared at the ceiling. A myriad of thoughts danced in my mind, competing for focus, but Stella could always bring order to the chaos.

"I only have three bedrooms and one doesn't have furniture. And I'd have to bring D.J. as well."

"I believe they've both slept in worst places than an air mattress in your spare room."

Tension began to ease, and I sat up straighter. "I suppose it would help me write my story. And I could stop going downtown."

Stella tapped a finger on my sleeve. "Hey, Clark Kent, put the reporter side of you away for once."

I smiled at her. "You want me to be Superman instead?"

She grinned "Mr. Fix-it. Here he comes to save the day."

"I believe that was Mighty Mouse. Get your superheroes straight."

"I'll try to catch a few more Saturday cartoons. What can I do to help you?"

I rested my head again, coming to terms with what was about to happen. Stella still held my hand in hers. I gave it a gentle squeeze. "I guess I'm doing this. You can do what you do best—help to keep us fed."

"I can do that."

"I'll pay you. No arguments." I freed my hand and stood, holding it out to help her up. "Walk over with me, and let's talk with Tyler."

We came up with a plan. We'd put Pete in the spare bedroom that Tyler was using, D.J. would camp on an air mattress in the office bedroom without any furniture, and Tyler would use my camping cot in the finished basement. He rather liked that idea since he'd have his own bath, TV, and space. Ginger would stay downstairs with Tyler most of the time to keep her out of Pete's way.

I hadn't talked with Pete and D.J. yet, but I suspected Pete would be released tomorrow. So Stella, Tyler, and I set out to move things around to accommodate the change.

"Someone's phone's ringing." Stella said.

"Can't be mine," Tyler said. "It's been shut off for months."

"Hello," I answered. "This is he."

I finished my call and shared the news.

"That was the Pittsburgh Police. Their undercover cop had some success. Two guys have been arrested. Description sounds like Jim, but he must have given you a false name. It should be on the news tonight." Tyler let out a whoop of delight. "Now I can move forward and try to do something with my life."

"Like work in my café?"

"Are you kidding?"

"Not kidding. I can use the help and you can have flexible hours while you go to school."

Tyler's head shot up in surprise, and he looked in my direction. "We talked about school, but I can't go yet. I need to work and get my own place."

I listened in on their dialogue.

She put her hands on her hips. "You can and will go to school. I see you pining over those brochures. There are grants and loans and scholarships. Think big."

"I don't know, Stella. I've gotta find somewhere to live."

"You don't like it here?" I joined the conversation.

Grinning, he said, "I like it here a lot. But I can't keep mooching."

"You planning to help with Pete? You planning to keep up the yard work you've been doing?"

"Yeah."

"So you're not mooching. Let me get Pete settled, and we'll look into some options next week." I still held my phone when it rang again. I answered, surprised to hear Caroline's voice on the line.

"I wanted to thank you again for taking me to that conservatory, and I'd like to show my appreciation by taking you to dinner."

Caroline showing appreciation? That seemed out of character and brought an amused smile. "Well that sounds great, but I have a few things going on, and I'll need to be close to home. Could we make that lunch? I could do tomorrow."

She named the restaurant and time that I should meet her.

"Thanks, Caroline. I'll see you then."

Tyler and Stella exchanged a look, and she moved toward the door. "If we're about done here, I've got stuff to do in my own house."

"Sure, Stel. Sorry if I kept you."

And with that she left.

Tyler ran his hands through his hair. "Man, that was cruel."

"What was cruel? What's with you two?"

"Aren't reporters supposed to have good intuition?"

"What am I missing here?"

He shook his head. "You're missing the boat, that's what."

He picked up the cot and headed downstairs.

I still didn't know what their cryptic secrets were and didn't have time to worry about it. I had to head back to the hospital. I owed D.J. some answers. I wanted some answers myself but had to let it go until we made plans for Pete. At some point, I'd learn the story about Andrew Bassett. Then I'd decide if I could merge his story with mine.

~*~

Alone in his room, Pete still looked weak but continued to be cheerful.

"Well howdee-do there, Scotty." His voice slogged from the sedation but didn't appear as weak as yesterday.

"How you doing, Pete?"

"Been better an' been worse."

"Where's D.J.?"

"He went on back to our place to get him some

sleep. Said they don't let 'em stay out in the waitin' room all night. He'll be back in the mornin'.'"

His hands tremored, his eyes glazed over. Was that the withdrawal, cancer, or sedation?

"Pete, what can I get for you? Anything to eat or drink?' Even in his weakness, his eyes opened wide. Wrong question.

"Can you sneak me in a little of my evenin' refreshment?" A twinkle lit his eye.

"Sorry, my friend. Can't do that. Coffee? Soft Drink? Anything else."

He waved me off with his hand. "I gotta be gettin' me outta here. I need to be a'gettin' home."

"We'll see what we can do, Pete. You rest up 'til morning. I'll be back."

I left the hospital and headed toward town. I'd hoped to never enter the little shed again, but I had to connect with D.J. tonight. I drove past the gatehouse, stopping for my ticket, and parked my car in the same lot that I'd sneaked into night after night. I pulled into a parking space close to the outbuilding.

Inside, D.J. was reading. He didn't seem surprised to see me. "Were you at the hospital?"

"Yeah. He's awake but groggy. Antsy to get out. He asked me if I could bring him some refreshment."

D.J. grinned. "He tried that on me, too."

I sat down on an old crate. "I guess I owe you some answers."

"I'd appreciate that." D.J. hoisted himself up to a sitting position.

I wouldn't mention that I'd considered including him in my project. That would spook him away for sure.

"I'm a writer. I'm doing a segment on

homelessness. Pete talked from the start, and I figured I'd get a lot of input from him. I didn't have to ask. He invited me along."

"So, you're here to help yourself...not for Pete." The old glare stole across his face but only lasted a moment. Pete's illness had moved us past that.

I didn't have a quick answer. I'd convinced myself of the altruism of the project, even while my goal was an award. No. In truth, the real goal was Charles Harrington's approval. Still, I felt the need to justify my project, perhaps to convince myself of its worthiness.

"Today I'm here for Pete. The old man has a way of getting to you. I'm looking at the shelters, the government programs, the social programs through churches and non-profs hoping to see what's there and what could be done better. I want to show that homeless people are real, generate some compassion."

D.J. looked straight at me without nodding his head or acknowledging my words. "Maybe some people aren't looking for compassion. Maybe some people want to be left alone."

"I don't think that describes Pete. He likes people."

"Pete tried to make the change when they took his daughter. When he couldn't do it, he accepted his life. He's not unhappy. Who else are you writing about?"

Careful... "I have a young kid that's been talking to me. He's had a rough life and couldn't seem to catch a break. Nice kid."

"That all?"

"That's all I've worked on."

"Did those investigative skills help you find Pete's daughter?"

"Yeah. I found her. That's a no-go. Pete guessed correctly that she wouldn't see him. She's pretty bitter. Has a lot of bad memories. And she has her hands full with a small house, pregnant daughter, and a toddler living there now. New baby's about to come. It's a definite no."

"I talked with the social worker. She can have Pete moved to the Veteran's Administration hospice care facility. Pete said he'll walk out. Do you think he will?"

"You know him better than I do. What do you think?"

"He'll walk. He wants his booze more than he wants those two months. One way or the other, he's out of Allegheny General."

"I have another option. I have a couple extra bedrooms. Why don't you two come with me for a little while?"

D.J.'s eyebrows rose with surprise. I caught the look before he went expressionless again—a skill he had mastered well.

"Pete's whole issue is the bourbon. He'll walk away from anywhere if he can't get his hands on it."

"What's the harm in letting him have his drink at this juncture of his life? It can't kill him before the cancer does."

"True. So you'd let him drink each night?"

"With supervision, so he doesn't hurt himself or my house."

"That's a generous gesture. Probably the best option he has. But there's no need to take me along. I'm going to have to get along without Pete at some point. Might as well be now."

"I'd be grateful if you'd agree to come. I can't always be there and you know Pete best. I don't know if I can do it without your help."

"So you'd take a complete stranger into your home?"

I chuckled. "I already have. The kid moved in with me. The street terrified him."

I wouldn't mention the drug deliveries that Tyler had once made. Tyler could share that or keep his secret.

"And I don't worry you at all?"

"How bad can you be when you read that every night?" I pointed to his Bible.

He slid it into his backpack and laid down.

"I'll think about it and let you know in the morning."

I had no intention of sleeping here tonight, but it felt awkward leaving D.J. alone.

"You want to come with me tonight? You can help move Pete there tomorrow?"

Without looking up, he said, "I told you. I'll let you know in the morning."

I stood from my makeshift seat, went to my car, and drove home. What in the world had I done?

23

Claire Bassett

Drew slept, so Isabella crawled into my bed for a story. We snuggled close in the tiny space.

Isabella snuggled into me and helped turn the pages. She had learned simple words, and when we came to one she knew, I would point and let her say it. Before too long, she'd be bringing primer readers home and reading to me. My little girl was growing up despite my distraction. So many hallmarks we should be celebrating. Moments Andrew shouldn't be missing.

The challenge of sharing a room surfaced most at bedtime and in the morning. Neither child had mastered the art of quiet. I finished the story and kissed the spiraled curls on top of her head resting on my chest.

"Let's go, Bella Love. Time for bed."

We tiptoed next door. She snuggled under the covers and whispered her prayers.

"When can we go back to our own house?"

"I don't know, baby. I hope it will be soon. Good night, little one."

The time had come to tell my parents. I hated the lies, and they already knew something was going on. I inhaled and offered a silent prayer.

Dad sat in his recliner, on the brink of dozing to

the drone of the TV. Mom was leafing through a gardening book. "Mom and Dad, can we chat for a few minutes?"

Dad muted the TV. "Sure can, Claire Bear."

I sat on the ottoman between them. "I know where Andrew is. He's living in downtown Pittsburgh—on the streets."

I let that sink in for a moment. Even my mother remained silent.

"I've been downtown trying to find him. He eats at a church that serves a free breakfast on weekdays. I went there today, but he didn't come in. That surprised the man who runs it because he comes every day. I plan to be there this Thursday, and every Tuesday and Thursday after that until I can find him."

Their silence became awkward.

"Say something, please. What are you thinking?"

"What can we do to help you?" Dad spoke first.

That didn't answer my question. They had been so angry with Andrew. I couldn't blame them. They'd watched us suffer emotional and financial hardship.

"You've done so much already. I don't know. Andrew needs help. I hope you know that this isn't him. He's not the kind of man who would leave us. He changed after...after the accident." It still hurt to give voice to it.

Dad took off his glasses and rubbed his eyes, looking his seventy years. "Would you like me to go with you? See if I can talk some sense into him?"

"Oh, Dad. Thank you, but I don't think it's that easy. I need to make him see that we can get the help he needs. I think it would be harder on him if you were there. He's always respected you so much. I think he'd be mortified for you to see him that way."

"Are you sure it's safe for you to go there?" Mom spoke for the first time.

"Yes, Mom. I've been there. It's a quiet place and it's in a church. I felt safe. I know you want to protect me and the kids, and I know you've been angry with Andrew for doing this. I get that because I've been angry at him, too. But I need to know that you'll forgive him, take him back as a son-in-law and a part of this family. Will you be able to do that?"

They turned toward each other and nodded their assent. It would be an act of their will, not their heart. They had witnessed my pain, had seen me struggling, had made sacrifices to help us. They saw how Bella, a daddy's girl, cried from missing him. The sad thing was that she missed him less and less as time went on. I had avoided talking to her about him in my attempt to lessen her pain. Perhaps it was time for me to change that.

"What will you do when you find him? Will you bring him here?"

Mom's question gave me pause. I hadn't thought through the details.

"Well, that will be hard for everybody, especially him, but I don't have any other options. I need to find a good counselor, one experienced with grief and guilt...survivor's guilt."

"I have some resources through the university. Would you like me to gather some names?"

"Thank you, Dad. That would help."

"Honey, Andrew is more than welcome here. But I think that you'll both need some space and some privacy. Think about this. The kids could stay here and we could get you and Andrew a month at an extended stay hotel with a little suite."

I nodded. "Maybe, Dad."

I rose and went to my mom, wrapping my arms around her. Dad stood and joined us. I hugged him and kissed his cheek. "Thank you, both. I couldn't do this without you."

Tomorrow would be another challenging day getting through work, trying to act normal. And I had to see Jonathan to cancel Saturday.

~*~

I walked the pathway toward the education building, my scarf shielding my face from the wind. It had taken some searching through boxes to retrieve winter gloves and a scarf. They were still packed up on my closet floor with the other things I needed but had no room for.

I made my way to my desk and peeled away the winter attire. My first task of the day: send Jonathan an e-mail asking to meet for lunch. It was too cold for the outside tables, so I suggested the Student Union Café.

He must have been sitting at his computer because the reply appeared within a minute. "Looking forward to it." A smiley emoticon followed.

~*~

By lunch time, my heart was in my throat. With leaden legs, I walked to Jonathan's office. He sat looking through his syllabus and there were heavy crowds of students there, too. I should have anticipated that. I didn't interact with them, but

Jonathan did.

However, he showed no signs of concern and stood when he saw me. "Hi there. I was pleasantly surprised when I got your e-mail."

"Do you have lunch? I brought mine with me."

"Yes." He retrieved his lunch bag from the front of his laptop case. "Feeling better today?"

"Not much. That's why I wanted to meet." I opened my bag and pulled the sandwich out. No appetite, though.

He grinned. "You mean it's not because of my irresistible charm?"

I gave him a sad smile. "You always have irresistible charm."

"I'm sensing a 'but' after that statement."

"But—but my life's a mess right now. I told you upfront that I'm married. There're some things going on that I need to attend to. I can't go out with you on Saturday."

A slow frown slipped over his face. His hand stretched across the table near mine. I met his reach and let his fingers enclose my hand. "OK. Someday next week?"

"No, Jonathan. I can't make any plans with you. I need to focus all of my attention on trying to save my marriage. Please understand. If I were single and free, I'd be thrilled to go out with you. But I'm not single, and I'm not free. I do want to thank you for the way you've made me feel. It had been a long time since I had done anything just for me. And I did enjoy myself."

He propped an elbow on the table and rested his head on his hand. "And if the marriage doesn't work?"

I closed my eyes against the thought. "My mind

can't go there."

"But if it doesn't?"

My eyes met his. "Would you really want my broken heart?"

This time he offered me a sad smile. "If that's the only way I could have it."

"I think we better eat our lunch before I start to cry."

~*~

Thursday morning, I arrived at St. John's by 6:00 AM. Without taking Drew to Molly's, I beat the heavy traffic. I didn't take Andrew's picture or ask anyone if they knew him. It had already been established that he chose this breakfast spot.

I arrived before anyone had come to eat. The smell of sausage greeted me, and I heard the popping sounds from the industrial-sized percolator. Don worked behind the counter, and I went over to say good morning.

"Did he come for breakfast yesterday?"

"No. Strangest thing. He's been here every morning for months. All of a sudden, he hasn't been here all week. You're welcome to wait."

"I can stay out of your way over there, or I'm happy to help if you need it."

"I never turn down free help. What's your name?"

"Claire. Tell me what to do."

I worked the free breakfast counter, serving, cleaning, and pouring coffee. I talked to the people I served, hoping someone had taken time to talk with Andrew, to treat him with respect and not see a street person. My eyes flew to the door every time it opened. Three and a half hours later, we locked up and cleaned up. I went into the ladies' room, where my cry turned to sobs. What do I do now?

I cleaned the tears from my face, although my red eyes betrayed me. As I waved good-bye and told Don I'd see him Tuesday, he walked over to the door.

"If you'd rather leave me a contact, I can call you when he's here, and you could run on in."

"I appreciate the offer, but I'm almost an hour away. By the time I got here, he'd be gone. I'll come each day I'm not working if that's OK with you. But would you mind calling me if he's here any other day when I'm not? It would help to know he's still in this general area."

"Write your phone number down here." He retrieved his own business card from his wallet. I glanced at it, wondering what job allowed him time every morning to serve breakfast to the masses. It said Program Director for the Pittsburgh City Outreach.

I jotted my name and number down and returned the card. "Thank you for what you're doing here. I have to confess I never gave much thought to the needs of homeless people 'til…well, until it hit home. Thank you. I'll be happy to help you each time I'm here."

"I'll be glad to take you up on that offer. I hope we find your husband."

"Thank you." I managed no more than a whisper.

24

Scott Harrington

I told D.J. he didn't worry me, but that wasn't entirely true. I didn't worry about my home or things. Money didn't motivate him. My gut told me he was OK, seeing his concern for Pete. But so many unknowns remained. Why leave that beautiful family? Why leave a good job?

In my mind, I kept seeing him staring at the little girl on the street corner, remembering the uncomfortable knot in my stomach. He could've been thinking of his daughter, or he could be a child molester. That would explain leaving his family and losing his job. But I made the offer, and he would let me know in the morning. There was no turning back.

As soon as I got home, I pulled out my laptop. While it powered on, I called downstairs to Tyler. "You can have the bed for one more night."

"I'm good here." He and Ginger cozied on the downstairs recliner, munching potato chips and watching TV.

I typed "Andrew Bassett" into my search engine. Finding information about him couldn't have been easier. Multiple sites appeared from the homepages of newspaper and news programs. One thing was certain. He had made news. I opened what I considered the most reliable source.

"The Allegheny County Coroners' office, along with the Pittsburgh Police, are investigating the death of a child. Three-year old Ellory Bassett was pronounced dead at Children's Hospital at 2:15 PM on Saturday, two hours after being struck by an automobile driven by Andrew Bassett, the child's uncle. The cause of death was blunt force trauma to the brain. The accident happened in the driveway of his Wexford home.

"No other passengers were in the vehicle. Bassett had been backing out of his driveway when the girl darted from her father and ran behind the moving car."

Another news article appeared, tucked into a smaller column the following week.

"Andrew Bassett, driver of the automobile that struck and killed his niece, Ellory Bassett, has been cleared of all charges. It has been ruled an accident."

I had enough background to lend some understanding to the trauma that sent Andrew Bassett over the edge, but still I dug to learn more about the man. I checked vital records and learned what I already knew—married to Claire Johnson Bassett, two children, senior accountant, MBA from the University of Pittsburgh, licensed CPA.

Growing up, he had two older siblings, Matthew and Leah. Matthew was the father of Ellory. He and his wife Jenny had no other children and had since divorced. Matthew relocated from Pittsburgh to Harrisburg after the accident.

I moved from the table to my sofa, closed my eyes, and tried to imagine the scenario, tried to bring life to a cold news article. I played the scene in my mind until it became too awful to see. Did Andrew see it every day? And what now? Should I turn my head and let him spend his life in a prison of his choice?

We had something in common...there were lots of ways to lose a brother. We'd both failed ours in grand fashion.

My eyes turned toward the clock. I needed Stella, but I couldn't call her this late. Still, I walked to my window and gazed across the yard, her house a shadow in the darkness. Her departure earlier today had been so abrupt. Had I said something to upset her? I couldn't think of what might have set her off.

With my mind on overload, sleep was out of the question. Pete, dying of cancer. D.J. suffering such a terrible trauma. The project, unwritten but filled with notes and potential.

Tyler was the one bright spot in this whole mess. I still wanted to locate Sam Pulkowski. Tyler opposed that idea, but there was always a story on both sides. Who would leave a kid like Tyler? Maybe someone self-absorbed and success-driven like Charles Harrington. But the article with Sam, the humanitarian work he did, his hand resting on his son's head—that didn't fit with someone self-absorbed. There had to be a story there. I should try to meet Sam. Size him up before deciding what to do.

I walked to the kitchen and stood at the window. A light came on next door. Stella must be sleepless tonight, too. Still, I couldn't call her at 1:00 AM. I felt like a voyeur. After about ten minutes, her house became dark again. I darkened my own and tried to sleep.

Morning sunlight invaded my drowsy eyes. They didn't want to open, but I stole a glance at the clock.

Nine eighteen. I lay there, recapping all I had discovered. I would be looking at D.J. with different eyes, and I feared he would see the truth in me. At some point, I would tell him I knew, but not yet.

"Hey Tyler, when did you learn to make coffee?" The delightful aroma of the fresh brew met me as I walked downstairs.

"You're forgetting I've had to take care of myself for a long time. Might surprise you what I can do in the kitchen."

"Look out, Stella. Competition." I reached for a mug and filled it.

"Well, not that good."

"I'm heading on down to the hospital as soon as I finish my coffee."

I peered around at my once quiet home. Tyler had brought some life to it, but soon, it would be chaos with four men and one dog sharing this space.

~*~

I entered Pete's hospital room, greeted by the antiseptic scent of sickness. D.J. had not yet arrived. The head of Pete's bed had been raised for him to sit, and his untouched breakfast remained on the tray. Pete loved to eat. I had breakfasted with him often enough at St. John's.

"What's up with this?" I pointed toward the tray of food.

"Go ahead and have yerself some. They gived me some medicine that turned my stomach against food. The quicker I get signed out, the happier I'll be."

"I think you're being released today."

"And I ain't goin' to one of them nursin' home places." He put on his best pout.

"Well, Pete, you can't go back to living on the street. So, I have a question for you. How would you feel about staying with me for a while?"

He tilted his head in confusion, staring like I had lost my mind. "Well, you's been staying with us, so iff'n I stay with you, that means we're all goin' back to my old shed."

I laughed. The old man was sharp, and I saw the amusement in his eyes. "What would you say if I told you I have my own home with a bed for you to stay in?"

"You go an' get you a job someplace?"

"I've always had a job, Pete. I'm a writer. I visited the shelters and hung out downtown to help me with a project. I'm writing a documentary about homelessness, and I'd like to write about you, if that's OK."

His mouth dropped open before it broke into a huge grin. "Well, howdee do! You sure had me fooled."

"So you're not angry that I didn't tell you?"

"You done told me right now."

"I guess I did. So, can I write about you?"

"Well, I'd be right honored if you do. So Ol' Pete will be famous?"

"Yeah, Pete, you'll be famous. Now, what about coming to stay with me?"

"Well, I'm right grateful, but I think I'll be headin' back to my own place."

"Pete, you don't have a place. That's a parking lot shed. Doctor said you can't go back there. I've got a warm home and a soft bed. Come on, and I'll bet D.J.'ll come too."

A little twinkle in his eye. "And I can have my

evenin' refreshment?"

"Don't worry. We'll keep you comfortable. I'll take you home, and we'll set up for the nurse to visit."

"Well, I thank ya kindly, Scotty. They was gonna try an' send me away somewhere." D.J. opened the door and peeked in. "Well, you hear that, Deej. We'll be a'goin' to Scotty's house."

"That so? How you feeling, old man?" D.J. walked toward the bed and looked at the untouched food.

"Well, my day got better. Do you know he's a writer fella, and I'm gonna be famous?"

Pete had a gift for making people smile.

"I'll go see to the paperwork and setting up the visiting nurse." I left them in the room with the assumption that D.J. would, indeed, be coming. It took about an hour to get everything signed and set up. I pulled the car up to the emergency entrance while a nurse escorted Pete down in a wheel chair. He sat in the front and D.J. climbed into the backseat. We started on our way without any other discussion from D.J.

At eleven forty-five, we pulled into the driveway to find Tyler and Stella sitting on the front step.

Stella jaunted over to the car to help, holding out her hand to D.J. first. "Hi, I'm Stella." She turned to Pete. "You must be Pete. I've heard a lot about you."

"Well howdie do, there. You Scotty's misses?"

Stella's head shot a glance my way. "No, Pete. I'm just his cook."

After introductions, I showed Pete and D.J. the spaces we had set up for them, while Stella set the table and laid out a variety of sandwiches, salad, and cookies. We walked toward the table, but Stella blocked my path.

"But not for you, Superman. Aren't you supposed

to be somewhere?"

I raised my eyes in question, showing my confusion.

"Lunch? Caroline?" She spoke the name with a level of disdain. "Downtown?"

Oh no—twelve fifteen and I had forgotten. I suspected Caroline McMann would not graciously handle being stood up. And I doubted she would be forgiving. My mind raced about what to do. Should I jump in my car and beg forgiveness for being late? Did I call and make up a lame excuse? I couldn't imagine she would still be waiting when I arrived, so I called instead and got her voicemail. Leaving a message was the only option.

"I had a minor emergency with a friend in the hospital. I'm sorry I missed getting that message to you earlier. I'll call you later today." I hung up.

Stella stood in front of me with her arms crossed.

"So now you're going to want me to feed you?"

I smiled. Surely, she was teasing as usual, wasn't she?

It turned out that Stella had plenty of food, which didn't surprise me.

While we ate lunch, D.J. looked around, sizing up the kitchen, the appliances, the TV, the recliner, as if he'd never been in a home before. How long ago had he left his? Would this scene prompt him to go home again?

Pete's face lit up at finding two new people to entertain with his stories. Stella met him story for story, beaming her radiant smile, while never looking in my direction. Pete got her laughter while I got the cold shoulder.

"Tyler, you OK here for a few minutes? I need to

talk with Stella."

He eyed me. "Yeah. You sure do."

Now what did that mean?

She cleared the table and started to clean dishes. "Hey Stel, I'll get that later. Can we sit outside for a minute? I need your ear."

She put down the dishtowel and walked out the front door without a word. I followed, sat on the step, and motioned for her to join me.

"What's wrong? Are you upset about something?"

She crossed her arms in front of her but then wrapped them around herself. "Why do you think that? I welcomed them, cooked for them, talked with them? What more did you want?"

"You were great with them. Are you upset with me?"

She was quiet for a moment. Her voice became gentle again. "No. I'm not upset with you."

I gave her a grin. "Could'a fooled me."

She turned toward me. "Problem's not you. It's me. Sorry. I shouldn't have been grouchy."

"Something I can do? Can I help with your problem?"

"Nope. Dreams and expectations. Sometimes I set them too high. Then I crash. Now, change the subject."

"But if…"

"I said to change the subject."

I got that message loud and clear. "I'd like to talk to you about D.J., but I don't want to leave Tyler alone this soon. Can I come over later, sometime early evening? Will you be home?"

She lingered, quiet for a moment before answering. "I'll be there waiting for you. It's what I do best."

25

Claire Bassett

On occasion, Pittsburgh experienced an October snow. It wouldn't last, since the roads were too warm to hold it for long. Under other circumstances, I would marvel at the beauty of the flakes drifting down. It created a surreal postcard scene where snow blended with the few remaining leaves that refused to fall from their branches.

But now the snow was an unwelcomed complication. My husband may be sleeping in a doorway or under a bridge. This first snowfall sent a visual notice that winter was on the move, waiting to attack with its usual vengeance. And if it lasted, I would have to drive in it before the road crews did their magic in order to be in town by 6:00 AM.

The time had come to make a phone call I'd been putting off for far too long. Before I found Andrew, I needed to know if Jenny or Matthew had come to a place of forgiveness. I dialed Jenny's number, and she picked up on the first ring.

My voice came out small and shaky. "Jenny? It's Claire."

There was silence for a moment.

"Claire, it's so good to hear your voice. I think of you so often."

I exhaled the breath I had been holding. "You don't know how relieved I am to hear that. I wasn't sure you'd want to hear from me."

"Oh, Claire, I should have contacted you. I've been working through a lot of things with the help of a counselor. The healing is slow, but it's coming. I'm still grieving, but it's a different kind of grief now. What about you? Did Andrew return?"

"No. I've moved in with my parents. I couldn't keep up with the house and couldn't sell it. I've rented it out for the time being." I hesitated and decided not to share where Andrew lived.

"I'm sorry. I have so much house here all to myself. You could have come here."

"It's better this way. I took a part-time job at the university and Mom helps with the kids. Jenny, tell me about Matthew. Any possibility for reconciliation for you two?"

"No. He's still bitter." The sadness trickled through her voice. "He blames me for going in the house and leaving him to carry the box from the car while watching Ellory. Believe me. I blamed myself for the longest time."

"And I suppose he still blames Andrew."

"He does. I'm sorry, Claire, but he's bitter. Refuses counseling. Said that doesn't help anything. You know he moved to Harrisburg?"

"No, I didn't know that."

"I think everything held too much pain. Me, this house that has Ellory's mark all through it, passing by your subdivision. Everything he couldn't handle. I guess you've had that, too, with Andrew leaving."

"I'm trying to find him, and I wanted to give him some hope that Matthew can forgive. I hated their last conversation. I know Andrew has relived that over and over."

I didn't voice the details. We both knew them, could still see Matthew pushing Andrew into the wall, yelling terrible accusations, saying it should have been our daughter, not his.

Jenny sighed. "I remember. I've had to talk with my counselor about that scene as well. If you find him, tell him I forgive him, from my heart. Andrew has no malice in him. And even though Matthew said those awful things, tell him it's not true—he is not a murderer, and..." A cry caught in her voice over the next words. "And it should not have been Isabella. It was an accident. A terrible, horrible, accident."

"Oh, Jenny. Thank you. I've missed you so much."

"Come see me, Claire. You are welcome anytime."

We hung up the phone, and I closed my eyes. "Thank You, God. Thank You."

I, too, should have sought counseling throughout this past year. It took all of my energy to focus on staying alive. But I'd lived through that accident, the scream, running from inside the house, seeing the blood soaking Ellory's baby-fine blonde hair, panic everywhere. I had been at the hospital when they declared her gone...I'd seen Jenny fall to her knees wailing, witnessed Matthew attacking my husband.

And in the three weeks that followed, Andrew had fallen into a deep depression. As I tried to repair all of the shattered pieces, I felt like Hans Brinker, the Dike Boy, trying to hold back the flood waters. When was there time for counseling?

Ellory. It had been a long time since I said her name. It tasted sweet on my lips. So pure, with a ready smile, the essence of innocence, and she was worth our tears.

My phone rang, pulling my thoughts back to now. I recognized the number I had saved to my phone. The name of my renters appeared, and I answered on the second ring, hoping there wasn't a maintenance problem.

"Everything OK with the house?"

"Oh, the house has been wonderful. We're so thankful we could stay here. And thank you for offering us a six-month lease. Those are hard to come by."

"Well, we've been helping each other. What can I do for you today?"

"We didn't expect this to happen so fast, but we found a house and we're set to close on it next week. It's vacant so the owner is anxious to have it done. I know we have four more months on our lease. We plan to pay that in full, but we'll be moving in two weeks."

Mixed emotions. I could have my home back, but then there'd be no rent. Even so, I didn't feel comfortable taking four month's rent from them when they wouldn't be there.

"That won't be necessary. I'll let you out of the lease."

"Absolutely not. My husband thought you might say that, and we both want to pay you. We made an agreement and will honor it."

How rare in this day and age.

Thoughts of home held such appeal. But what about Isabella's school? And my furniture in storage? I couldn't go home and absorb the expense of moving, only to look for new renters and do it all again. No, the house would have to stay vacant. I'd place an ad next week.

26

Scott Harrington

After trying to call Caroline three times with no answer, I put it out of my mind. She must be majorly upset and screening her calls.

Pete and D.J. had settled in and didn't seem to require much of me. Pete wouldn't hang on much longer, so time had become a precious commodity. And soon, I would need to contact Sam Pulkowski and Claire Bassett. Those two bios could not be complete until I made the connections. I hoped for some happy endings.

I had to get writing. For now, I would concentrate on Pete and getting waivers signed. I could get signatures from Pete and Tyler, and soon I would have to talk with D.J.

All three of them stood on the deck, watching the snow fall from a night sky. They were so accustomed to the cold that it didn't have much impact. D.J. lifted his head and inhaled the scent of winter's approach. I stepped out to join them.

"It's cold out here. None of you have a jacket on."

"It'll be gettin' a load colder 'fore too long. It'll be right nice to be in this house when ol' man winter comes a'callin'."

Pete may not be around to see old man winter's arrival. Would he even make it to Thanksgiving? We'd plan as if he would and accept what came.

"We're going to have to plan a Thanksgiving dinner together. Who knows how to cook a turkey?"

Tyler turned his head toward me and responded. "Stella. That's who."

"Sorry, buddy. I believe she'll be visiting family that weekend. We'll be the four bachelors."

D.J. spun around, but he swallowed whatever words threatened to escape. I could've kicked myself for that blunder. "I guess we'll be reading some cookbooks. We'll divide and conquer. Anyone have any special cooking skills?"

"I ain't much of a cook, but I might could find us a beverage." Pete's eyes shone with delight. "'Course I'd be a'needin' my signs and a corner in this here town first."

We all got a chuckle out of that. He wouldn't be on a Sewickley corner two minutes before a cop got to him.

"Tell you what, Pete. You get a pass since you just got out of the hospital. Tyler, what can you cook?"

"I've done mashed potatoes before, but I can't make gravy."

"Done. Heinz makes a great jar of gravy. D.J., you got any culinary skills?"

His expression went slack, and he stared at his hands. After an awkward moment of silence, he looked up and managed a half grin. "Well, I've been known to roast a turkey. And forget buying gravy. I can make that as well."

Everyone gave a whoop of delight. We had a cook, yet my stomach knotted at the look on D.J.'s face. I had to try to get D.J. home where he belonged, before this family spent the holiday season apart.

"Pete, if you still want to be a celebrity, can I get you to sign a paper giving me permission?"

"Sure can. Get me a pen."

"Tyler, how about you?"

He shook his head and crossed his arms. "Told you I want to read it first."

"Fair enough. Trust me. You'll love it." His story had potential. We needed to start looking into college. That would ice the cake.

I sat down in my new makeshift office. My bedroom had become my sanctuary for writing without distractions. I would watch the clock and head over to see Stella by seven. I started my exposé on Pete Simmons, beginning with his childhood, marriage, service, wild weasels, POW, poor treatment from the culture at large when he came home, and his fall into alcoholism.

"Scott. Come here. Quick." Tyler called from the bottom of the stairs.

I bolted. Was Pete having a medical crisis? But the TV had become the focal point. Holding the remote to the DVR, Tyler reversed the newscast, finding the spot he wanted. The words of the anchor sounded while the video showed Caroline being escorted from her office into a police car.

"Caroline McMann, a receptionist for Three Rivers Missions, has been implicated in a drug ring. There were two arrests made earlier this week. John Hilleman and Leo Holder have since turned evidence against Ms. McMann, stating that she organized and supplied the drugs that were imported from Mexico, traveling through Charleston Harbor. A search warrant turned up spreadsheets and a journal with names and dates."

The video changed to an image of another police car, and the voice-over continued. "Also taken into custody is Jeffrey Cook, financial manager for Clearway Rehabilitation Center in Greensburg. Clearway Rehab is a facility for teenagers and young adults who battle addiction. It is an affiliate of the Three Rivers Missions."

My jaw dropped. I moved closer, taking in the scene. Stella rapped before opening the door to find us all gazing at the TV.

"I guess you saw? Is that your girl?"

"That's her." Tyler answered for me. "Did you see that coming?"

"Not in a million years." I shook my head. "I called the connection with the rehab, but Caroline? I didn't see that coming."

I shook my head again, as if that could change what had occurred. I had asked Caroline about drugs. She'd given a vague answer, and her demeanor had changed rapidly. But then, she changed demeanors quicker than a flash of lightning.

Caroline harbored so much resentment for Ray Brockman and for having responsibilities unequal to compensation. She'd been accustomed to abundance yet disowned by her family. Would she do anything to maintain that lifestyle?

I'd grown up with abundance, but I loathed the deception of that way of life.

Stella stepped behind me and put her hand on my shoulder, her mouth close to my ear. "Sorry, Scott. Guess you saw what you wanted to see."

Tyler rewound again, muted the voice-over, and

played the video, pausing on a full shot of Caroline. "Looks like a socialite. Not your type."

I stared at the stilled shot of Caroline. "And how would you know my type after knowing me for all of six weeks?"

"I could see you going for someone more down to earth, sort of a girl next door type."

I continued staring at the paused TV. "You forget. I grew up in an isolated mansion. We had no girls next door."

Tyler shook his head, put down the remote, and walked away.

Stella turned to leave. "I'm outta here. Just wanted to make sure you saw it."

"Thanks, Stel. Did you remember I'm stopping over later?"

"I remembered. You're not that forgettable, Harrington."

"See you in about half an hour."

They all dispersed, and I stood there. Caroline. I shook my head. "Unbelievable."

Going back to the bedroom office, I pulled up the news articles I'd located regarding D.J. and the accident, bookmarked them, and went to another search engine. I typed Claire Bassett into the browser. Once again, the same news articles surfaced, but I managed to find an address. She lived in Wexford, a short drive from here. I found a phone number and again faced the decision—call or drop in for a surprise visit.

How would Claire Bassett react to word of her husband? Perhaps the accident came on the heels of other issues. She may have thrown him out and wouldn't welcome news of his whereabouts.

Gathering all of my findings and all of my questions, I left Tyler tending to our houseguests and went to see Stella.

In the thirty minutes since she had left my house, she had unpinned her hair. I was accustomed to seeing it pulled back and secured with a net, and it always took me by surprise when I saw it down. Long and light blond, she had brushed it to a smooth glow that accentuated natural highlights. She was a beauty. Why had she never married? For the two years I had known her, she hadn't dated anyone with regularity.

"Hope you're full of wisdom tonight, 'cause I have some heavy stuff here. I need to make some decisions."

"Sofa or table?"

The table would have been more practical, but the thought of a soft place to land tempted me.

"Sofa. I'm weary." I sank into the soft comfort, an old-fashioned patchwork quilt tied with yarn thrown over the arm rest. Among the array of magazines lined on the coffee table, two of them published my work. Both had an author picture following my article.

I picked up one and smiled. "You still have this?"

She plucked it from my hand and returned it to the spot. "I like the recipes."

She sat beside me, and I laid the laptop between us.

"Read. Nod when you're done, and I'll open the next."

As Stella read the article about the accident, she gasped, covered her mouth, and then wiped a drop of moisture from the corner of her eye. She nodded. "Go on."

I pulled up the next article, followed by details about D.J.'s family and a photo of Claire that I found online.

We sat side by side, silently, until Stella asked the question that I had pondered. "What are you going to do now?"

"I thought I'd ask a wise café owner for advice."

"Oh, Scott. He needs help." She placed her hand on my arm.

"I know. But does he know that? It's hard to be helped until you know you need it."

"Does he know you have all this information?"

"No. Not sure if I should talk with him first or go see the wife. What if she's hostile toward him and kicked him out? I'd make matters worse by trying to talk him into seeing her."

"I guess you have your answer. Go see the wife first."

I laid my head back and squeezed the bridge of my nose, which did nothing to alleviate the tension. "How do I get myself involved in these things? I only wanted to write a documentary."

"People come with messy stuff. It's never neat and cozy when you look deep."

My head rested on the sofa cushion behind me, my hand covering my eyes. Stella touched my hair, smoothing it back. My street days were over. I could get a decent trim. Such a useless thought among the weighty issues.

"I've got to go see Caroline. She needs to know what she's done, needs to know about kids like Edwin. Did she ever see the lives, the faces? Was money worth the cost?"

The changes in Edwin had happened so fast. The big brother I could always count on withdrew. His mood swings were like a roller coaster, and then the light went out of his eyes. How was it that no one noticed? Had I been the only one looking?

My voice cracked, and I covered my face to hide my weakness. "Was it worth the guilt of those left behind?"

Stella put her arm over my shoulder and drew me closer.

"Scott. Look at me." She touched my hands to move them from my face. "Look at me."

I obeyed. Her face held compassion.

"You were fifteen years old. You were a child—a child placed in a terrible situation. You'd lost the intimacy with your brother, the only person you'd ever had a relationship with. You had a domineering father and an absent mother. Don't carry this burden of guilt. It's not yours. Put it where it belongs. Your brother made bad choices. Your parents didn't parent well. A fifteen-year-old kid can't be expected to handle the gravity of that situation."

I put my arms around her and leaned into her softness, the blond hair whispering lavender against my face. I felt her tension release, and she melted against me. My lips brushed her cheek but then I caught myself, unwilling to allow my vulnerable state to ruin our friendship.

As I pulled back, she kept her head down. I tipped her chin upward with my hand.

"Stel, what would I do without you?"

Her eyes were moist, creating a reflection pool in which I could see myself— my weakness.

"What do you want, Scott? I mean, really want?"

"I guess I want to fix everybody. But I can't seem to fix myself. I can't forgive myself. I haven't seen my father in two years. I have little respect for the man. So why is his approval so important?"

"Because he's your father. It's a bond that's not easy to break. You can create distance in your life but not in your heart. It might be time for a visit."

I nodded. "We'll see."

But that wouldn't happen. Not without a Pulitzer in hand. I stood to walk to the door, and Stella walked with me.

"Thank you. You always help me to see things more clearly."

She brushed my hair back. "You know, sometimes what we want is right before our eyes."

She moved her hand to my face and placed a soft kiss on my cheek.

Later that evening, I dialed the number of the Wexford home of Claire Bassett. It had been disconnected. That gave me only one option.

I would pay a visit to the Bassett home.

27

Scott Harrington

I knocked on the door of D.J.'s bedroom. He had stretched out on the air mattress with a book.

"Can we talk?"

"Sure. Is it Pete? Is he worse?" D.J. closed his book and stood up.

"No. Not about Pete."

I opened the closet door and pulled out a folding chair. Turning it backward, I straddled the seat, motioning for him to sit in the one easy chair I kept in the room. I needed to get a sense of his state of mind before contacting his wife. I wouldn't tell him I intended to see her, but I had to get some perspective from him first.

"D.J., I know your real name. I know a little about your situation."

He gave a pensive nod. "The accident?"

I leaned in, resting my arms on the chair's back. "Yeah, the accident."

We sat in silence for a moment. D.J.'s eyes looked past me, though there was nothing to see but a blank wall. It took me back to St. John's the day I asked him what he did before living on the street.

I waited out the silence, and he again met my eyes.

"I figured you knew. You're a reporter. Didn't expect you'd let me in your house without checking me out."

"So do I call you D.J. or Andrew?"

He rested his head back, much like I had done last night at Stella's. "I don't know anymore. I've been a different person this year, out there on the street. But being here, in a house with other people, part of me is starting to remember how it felt to live."

We had come a long way from that first grunted introduction over breakfast. "How can I help you? What took you away from home?"

He placed his elbows on his knees and rested his chin on his folded hands for a long time. Had he shut himself off again? Did he plan to answer? Then he turned back to me.

"I don't expect anyone to understand this. Heck, I can't understand it myself. Everywhere I looked, I saw pain. Pain so deep it became physical, like it stabbed me right in the heart. I couldn't walk outside my house without seeing the spot where it happened. My chest burned like I wasn't getting enough air. I couldn't look at my daughter. I love her so much that the thought of something like that happening to her would kill me. I'd look at her and know that's what I did to my brother. I couldn't hold my wife and know how much we loved each other when I'd destroyed my brother's marriage."

He turned an agonized expression downward. I shared that level of pain. Someday I might tell him.

"I guess on top of that, I walked around, still walk around, every day with the guilt. I should have been punished, but the legal system didn't punish me."

I nodded my understanding. "So you punished yourself."

"I had to. How could I go back to normal life like

nothing happened? Matthew didn't have that option. There had to be punishment."

Another emotion we shared. The guilt still stabbed at me when Edwin's face—forever young as I grew older—crossed my mind.

I pointed to the book on the floor beside the air mattress, tattered and worn from use. "What does your Bible say about that?"

D.J. grinned, such a rare sight. "It says I'm forgiven. But that's then. In the big picture. Here on this earth, there should be consequences."

"I'm not sure I've ever read that part."

"Well, it just makes sense."

I could philosophically argue that point, but it would be counterproductive. "What now? Do you want to go home?"

"More than anything in the world. But I can't do that."

"Why? Same reasons that you left? There are some better options than the parking lot shed."

"No. Different reasons. How can I walk back in after what I've done to my wife and kids? I abandoned them. I couldn't handle the guilt and now I've added more guilt on top of that. I can't go back like nothing happened. I'm sure they've all moved on by now."

"How would you feel about getting some help?" My hands formed a steeple resting on the chair.

"You mean counseling?"

"That's a start."

He shook his head. "No. No money and I won't panhandle. And when Pete's gone, I'm headed back downtown. I won't live off you."

"D.J., I can't let you do that." Even I heard the sadness in my voice.

He grinned that half-grin again. "You really don't have anything to say about it."

"I can help you."

He seemed to be considering. Had I broken through a small part of the wall he'd built around himself? Pete had, so there was still the basic human need to care and be cared for.

"You're a good man. Thanks for what you're doing for Pete, and for wanting to help me. Let's get through this thing with Pete. He's getting weaker all the time. Some days he doesn't want to get out of bed anymore."

"The hospice nurse will be here this morning."

I left D.J., hoping he'd consider another path. In the meantime, I would contact Claire Bassett. It didn't sound like a hostile break up.

After spending the rest of the day writing, I spent more time looking for people in cyber space. Sam Pulkowski lived in the South Hills, a short ride across town.

Tomorrow would be a busy day. I planned to pay a visit to Claire Bassett in Wexford, Sam Pulkowski south of the city, and Caroline McMann in the county jail. I needed some fresh air and walked over to update Stella.

~*~

The clock said 6:00 AM, but too many issues competed in my brain. Along with the constant sound of coughing from Pete's room. My body refused to go back to sleep.

I got up and set up the coffee. The sun started to rise without much promise—gray and threatening.

It was way too early to head out, so I opened my laptop to put final touches on two of the bios, but it was hard to concentrate with the sound of Pete's constant cough.

I walked over and knocked before opening his door. He lay there, wracked with cough. The sallow complexion alarmed me. He had become a skeletal form of his old self.

Should I call 9-1-1? But what would they do? This was hospice care. We all knew how it would end.

"Hey, Pete. You OK?"

He held out his hand, a gesture that required much exertion. I took it and sat beside him, breathing the sick-sweet scent in the air.

"Scotty, I thank ya kindly for this here bed."

The energy expended for those words led to more coughing. The trash receptacle beside the bed overflowed with bloody tissues.

"I'm honored to have you here." Words passed through the thickness in my throat.

"I don't aim to be here much longer, Scotty. I think the good Lord is callin'."

"You right with Him, Pete?"

"I'm hopin' so. D.J.'s been talkin' to me 'bout that. Tells me things that's in that Bible of his. We done talked to Him together."

"You keep doing that, Pete. He's good to His promise."

"I'm fixin' to see that promise pretty soon."

No reason to deny it. He knew. We all knew. "We're here with you."

Pete reached for my hand again and curled his fingers around mine. The strength in his grip surprised me, but the voice was a whisper. "Take care of my boy,

Scotty."

I tilted my head. "Your boy?".

"Deej. My boy. Lots troubling him."

I nodded. "I'll watch out for him, Pete. You've got my word."

He closed his eyes and drifted into a rasping sleep.

At 9:00 that morning, I placed a call to Mary Anne Marshall.

"I wanted to update you. We brought your father to my home to ride out the end of this illness. The hospice nurse agrees we're looking at the last few days. I wanted you to know."

"Has he asked for me to come?"

How do you tell a daughter that he hasn't asked for her? Dodge the question. "He's medicated—in and out of sleep. I wanted you to have information. I work from home, so the address is on my business card. You're welcome to come anytime. I understand if you can't."

"Thank you for the call. I'll think about it."

I hung up and went downstairs to talk with Tyler.

"Hey Ty. I've got to go out today. Some important tasks. Pete's going down fast. Will you stick around here?"

"Sure. I'll call if there's anything to tell. And, Scott, thanks for reactivating my phone. I promise I'll pay you back someday."

"Not worried about that. I'm more worried about you here alone with no phone and a dying man. I'll be back as soon as I can."

~*~

A gray chill covered the city as I drove to Wexford,

but at least the snow held off. The Bassett home was located in a subdivision that consisted of beautiful, stately homes. Tasteful—not the pretentious estate I'd escaped.

I parked on the street and walked up the sidewalk. Pausing, I swept my gaze toward the driveway. I imagined the scene, and it chilled me more than the cold of winter. No wonder he couldn't stay.

I rang the doorbell twice, but no one answered. As I walked back to my car, two ladies wearing scarves and mittens approached me.

"Can we help you?" Long blond hair extended beyond the knitted cap.

"I'm looking for Claire Bassett. Is this the right house?"

They flashed a guarded look at each other.

"I'm Molly, her neighbor," the brunette answered, her cheeks red from the cold. "This is her home, but she's not here. Why don't I take your name and have her call you?"

I could do that, but I always liked the ball in my own court.

"Could you tell me a good time to come back? I'm sure she'll want to talk to me."

The blonde introduced herself. "I'm Jan. We're friends with Claire. Can you tell us what this is about?"

I wasn't about to tell them much. "It's about her husband."

They exchanged a look. "She isn't here now. She's staying with her parents."

"How can I find her?"

"Slippery Rock. She works at the university."

They declined to share an address, so that would have to do. I could locate her parents, but it might be better to see her alone.

My failure at finding anyone home gave me some hesitation about visiting Sam Pulkowski. Chances would be better of finding him home in the evening. I sat in my car and pulled up Slippery Rock University's website on my cell phone. It listed employee extensions, and I dialed the number in the School of Education noted for Claire.

"School of Education, Claire Bassett speaking."

"Sorry, wrong number." I hung up the phone and headed north toward Slippery Rock.

28

Claire Bassett

The calendar had turned to November, my second Thanksgiving without Andrew.

It was too cold for Isabella to wait at the bus stop, so I drove her to school. The wind whistled through my loose car window. I'd need to have that repaired. My spirits matched this gray, agitated day. Like the wind, I moved without going anywhere. Icy fingers of cold attacked my windshield, requiring my defrosters to dissolve them. Would anything soften the icy fingers grabbing at my heart?

Every visit to St. John's came up empty, so I'd decided not to return. Don promised to call should Andrew appear. Until then, I waited, married but with no husband, unsure if it was better or worse knowing he lived on the streets. It had torn me apart when I thought he could be dead. Yet knowing he was out there, wasting away and freezing…I couldn't erase that image from my mind.

Pulling up to the drop-off, I helped Bella retrieve her little backpack, kissed her good-bye, and watched her walk the isolated path to the early arrival room. A caregiver waited at the door to greet her, waved to me, and then they disappeared into the red brick building.

The office became a distraction from the horrors of my life. My coworkers may have thought me to be aloof, but I had fallen into the pattern of keeping to myself. Forming friendships and making small talk always led to discussions I didn't want to have.

Jonathan was a perfect gentleman, and I was grateful. "Hey, Claire. Did your kids like seeing the snow?"

We made small talk. That's what we did these days. He continued to touch base with me often but had stopped any form of flirting. He no longer mentioned dinner or touched my hand. And yet, the touch of another person would have gone a long way toward melting the ice forming around my heart.

A few minutes of small talk and he walked back to his office, his absence increasing the melancholy that followed me to work that day.

A few hours later, I heard my name mentioned at the front desk.

"I'm looking for Claire Bassett." The voice belonged to a man.

"Claire's desk is back there, last one on the left."

I heard the clunk of footsteps before I saw him in my limited cubicle view. A well-dressed man, tall with a clean look and a dimpled chin.

I stood as he approached. "I'm Claire. Can I help you?"

"My name is Scott Harrington. Is this a good time and place to talk with you?"

I eyed him with suspicion. "Regarding?"

"Regarding Andrew."

While I felt the skip in my heartbeat, I still approached this conversation with reservation. If he'd come to tell me Andrew was homeless and freezing on the streets, I already knew that.

I motioned to the door he'd just entered. "Let's go somewhere more private." I led the way, and he followed. Walking past the front desk, I called to Susie. "I'm taking a short break. I'll be back soon."

We continued to an empty conference room used for student advisement. I motioned to the chair.

"Please, sit. Do you know Andrew? Do you know where he is?" While desperate for the answer to that question, I remained guarded.

"He's at my home, staying with me. Temporarily."

My eyes betrayed me as they pooled with unshed tears. I covered my mouth. I had lost the ability to form words into a logical thought.

"He's hurting, Claire. He needs help."

I nodded, recovering from the shock. Of course he needed help. "Does he want help? Is he ready for it?"

"Yes, he is. He doesn't know I'm seeing you. He's convinced you've moved on and that he can't return."

"When can I see him? I can leave here now."

"I think tomorrow would be better. There are some things I have to do today that are taking me away from home."

"I'm afraid he'll disappear if I wait."

Scott wore a burdened look. "He won't disappear."

I would have said the same thing a year ago. "Please don't let him leave. My biggest fear is he'll run again."

"He won't run. He's befriended an old man who's at my house getting hospice care. D.J. won't run out on Pete."

But he ran out on me. "D.J.? Is that what he calls himself?"

"Yeah, it's what he's been going by."

"Drew. Our baby. He's sixteen months old now. Those are his initials. We debated whether to call him Andrew, Jr., D.J., or Drew. We decided on Drew."

He pulled out his wallet and retrieved a business card. "Here's the address. What time do you want to come? I'll arrange some privacy."

"Nine? I can drop Isabella at school and come from there."

"Nine it is."

"Will he know? Are you telling him we met?"

He appeared to ponder that and shook his head.

"No, Claire. Let's just do it. I think the element of surprise would be better. If he knows, he'll spend a lot of time worrying."

As he left the conference room, I clasped my hands in front of my face. This is what I'd hoped for. It would happen tomorrow.

~*~

I packed my things to leave early. I didn't know what would become of my job. Once I had Andrew in my grips, I'd be afraid to leave him.

I glanced around my little cubicle, my refuge from the reality of life. The plaque still sat atop the desk. *The earth laughs in flowers*. Maybe spring would come.

Who knew what tomorrow held. I should see Jonathan before I left. His schedule said that he had office hours right now. He may have had a student meeting with him, but I took the chance and walked up the hallway that held the professors' offices. He was alone in his office and working at his computer.

He glanced up at the slight rap on the door, his

eyes widening. He gave a tentative smile. "Well this is a pleasant surprise."

I pulled his windowless office door until it clicked. "Mind if I sit for a few minutes?"

Without answering, he came out from behind his desk and sat in the chair across from me. "Do you think I would ever mind that?"

I smiled at his sweetness, not sure how to begin.

"Are you OK, Claire? I've been worried about you."

That exemplified Jonathan, his sweet caring nature. "I think so. A lot of things are going on right now. I feel like I owe you an explanation."

"You don't owe me. But I'm here if you want to talk about it."

"I do. There's so much you don't know. I'll start with my daughter's fifth birthday party. We had a small family gathering. An hour before the rest of our family planned to arrive, my brother-in-law and sister-in-law came early to help me set up. We were close in those days. "

Jonathan listened as I rambled on. "I thought we might need more ice cream, so I asked Andrew to run to the store before anyone else came. Matthew and Jenny were arriving. Jenny came into the house. Her daughter, Ellory stayed out with her dad."

I squeezed my eyes against the scene about to come. "I never heard the hit, but I heard Matthew screaming. Jenny darted out the door before me, and her screams followed."

Jonathan leaned forward, his elbows on his knees.

I went on to tell him the horrid details. "When the doctor said she was gone, Matthew went crazy. He attacked Andrew, pushed him against the wall, and called him a murderer. He said it should have been his own daughter, my Bella."

Jonathan reached for my hand, shaking his head against the awful picture.

"Andrew wasn't held liable. The investigation called it an accident. But he went downhill, every day for three weeks. The deepest depression held him, he stopped talking, and sometimes didn't get out of bed. After three weeks, he disappeared."

I told him the rest, the cell phone picture, canvasing the city, St. John's. And today's visit from Scott Harrington. I would be seeing Andrew tomorrow and hoped to bring him home.

We both knew this meant the end of any possibility of a future. And yet sweet Jonathan, who for some reason adored me, was the most gracious friend.

"I am so, so sorry for all you've been through. I wish you'd told me sooner. You know how I love my little niece, Hannah. I can't fathom being in that position. I may have done what your husband did. What can I do to help you, Claire?"

"You have done more than you will ever know. I have something I want to give you."

I reached into my pocket and retrieved the note I, for some unknown reason, had kept. I handed it to him and he read aloud his own words. "You brought light into my darkness."

Looking puzzled, he said, "I wrote this for you."

"Yes, and those are the exact words I want to say to you. You kept me going, kept shining light into my dark world. I'm giving that back so you'll know what you've meant to me."

Our eyes locked until I stood. "I need to go. Thank you for being you."

I stepped into his hug. He held me, brushed his lips across my cheek. I separated from the closeness. I was a wife, and my husband waited. He walked me to the office door, held it open, and squeezed my hand.

"Good-bye Claire. I'll be praying for you and for your husband."

~*~

I told my parents that night but refused to have them accompany me. Instead, they entertained the kids that evening.

Once in my bedroom, I hit the floor with my knees, folded my hands, and rested them on the side of the bed.

"Lord, please, please let him still be there. Help me to find words to say, words to show him there's help and hope. To show him how much I love him. Ready his heart to see me. Let him know the reality of forgiveness. Yours, mine, and Jenny's."

29

Scott Harrington

The Allegheny County Jail sat in the heart of downtown. I had only been inside once, while doing an interview. Walking in the main door, I supplied my photo ID and emptied all of my belongings—wallet, cell phone, belt, coins—everything came out of my pockets before walking through the security scanner. I kept two small items tucked in my shirt, hoping they wouldn't be noticed and confiscated.

A guard escorted me to the visiting room through two sets of electronic doors that opened and locked at his command. The guard left me alone and the door lock clicked behind him. I scanned the small visiting area, noting a small table and chairs, and multiple cameras aimed at a variety of areas. A visitor couldn't move more than two feet without being in some camera's view.

Thirty minutes passed before a female guard escorted Caroline in. Her thick hair was pulled back and secured with a band. Leg shackles peeked through the base of her orange jumpsuit, and handcuffs held her arms in front as she walked. One sculpted eyebrow rose as she saw me, but neither of us spoke before she sat down.

The guard removed her handcuffs but secured her

leg shackles to a loop on the floor. She moved away but never left the room. Caroline massaged her wrists where the cuffs had rubbed. I noticed her flawless red nails. That would be her last high-end manicure for a while.

She spoke first, breaking the silence. "Why are you here?"

"I missed our last date." My attempt at humor fell flat, and she remained silent. I moved on, letting it pass. "Why, Caroline? I need to know why."

She focused on her wrist, rubbed it, turned it over, and moved her hand back and forth to stretch the joint. Then she glanced up. "You're assuming I'm guilty?"

"Are you?"

She shrugged. "My attorney has counseled me to keep my mouth shut."

"A difficult task for a sassy young lady." I leaned in closer. "Was it the money? The power? What?" My head tilted with each question.

Stone silence.

I glanced at the guard, who paid no attention to us, and pulled out the two pictures.

"I want you to see this." I turned the first picture toward her.

"Is that you?" She pointed to my image.

"Yeah, me at ten years old."

"And your friend?"

"My brother, Edwin. Fourteen months older than me."

"Cute. And why do I need to see this?" Snarky even in her prison garb.

I turned the next one face up and rotated it toward her.

"This is Edwin's school picture in his sophomore

year. I don't have a photo of his junior year. He OD'd three days before they were taken."

She glanced and turned away. Typical. No one wanted to see the faces behind the crime.

"Look at it." My voice filled with agitation as I pushed the photo closer. "That's what you did. Lured kids into that lifestyle, supplied them with lethal chemicals that ruined and stole their life. Did you ever think of that when you padded your bank account?"

She turned toward the guard, showing no emotion, no remorse. Lifting a hand, one finger extended, she summoned her as she had done with our waiter. "Guard, I'm ready to go back."

I ran my hands through my hair and shook my head.

The guard came over and reattached her handcuffs. Another escorted me through the doors that automatically locked behind me.

I left the jailhouse feeling more frustration than before. I wanted her to know there were kids dying, kids with families who loved them and brothers that would be forever consumed by the guilt of living.

I couldn't go home where I'd face people who could read my mood, where I'd hear Pete dying, cough by painful cough, and where I'd see D.J. and wonder what tomorrow would bring.

As I drove around, aimlessly crossing bridges, I made my way to the Fort Pitt Tunnel just so I could cross back to the spectacular view. Exiting the tunnel onto the Fort Pitt Bridge, the magnificent city skyline greeted me. It had been penned as the best way to enter an American city. The familiar sight somehow brought clarity to my muddled thoughts.

Turning again, I entered the Liberty Tube and

made my way to the South Hills. I'd ride past Sam Pulkowski's home to locate it. I had no expectation that he would be there on a workday, but I plugged the address into the GPS and headed south.

The directions took me to a small neighborhood in the community of Dormont. The houses were dated, but it appeared to be a well-kept street. The hilly terrain elevated most of the two-story brick homes, requiring a long, outside stairway to reach the porch. I stopped in front of the house and parallel parked along the street.

A worker was cutting spindles to replace some on the front porch. I jaunted up a few steps and called toward him.

"That's looking good. You live here or work here?"

"Both. I live and work here. You're never done when you own a home. Can I help you with something?"

"Scott Harrington." I ascended the stairs and reached out to shake his hand. "I saw you working and thought I might get a business card. I guess if this is your own place, you don't do this work for others."

"I do, and I can give you a card. Most jobs are bigger, new home construction, but if I can fit you in, I'll give it a try. What are you needing?"

No more deceit. I glanced at his business card. It did indeed read "Sam Pulkowski."

"Sam Pulkowski. You have a son named Tyler?"

With that, he stood up. "You know Ty? You know where he is?"

"I do. He's staying with me, trying to get his life together."

He removed his tool belt, and tossed it onto the

porch. "I need to see my boy."

"Hold on a few minutes. Let's talk."

"Hey, I've been looking for that kid since his mother snatched him out of my grasp ten years ago. She didn't stay in one place long enough to give him any roots. No trail to trace. I'm ready to see him now."

I made a downward gesture with my hands to indicate we needed to take this slower. "Tyler doesn't know that. He thinks you abandoned him."

"Abandon Ty? He knows better."

"No. Actually, he doesn't know. He was nine and you never came back. That's all he knows. You're aware that his mother moved to Texas?"

"No. I didn't know. But he's here? How'd he hook up with you?"

"Tyler lived among the homeless men in Pittsburgh. It scared him to death. I'm trying to help him find a way out."

Sam turned from me and kicked his work boot into a stack of wood, scattering it over the floor of his front porch. I took a step backward, but his anger was not at me.

"I should've taken him when I left. I had nowhere to live and wanted to get settled. I went back for him in three weeks, and they were gone. I never should've left without him."

"Sam, he's a great kid. Smart, respectful. Right now, he's at my place, helping to take care of an old man who's dying of lung cancer. Not many eighteen-year-olds up to that task. I've grown fond of him."

"Can I see him? I don't want to wait." His eyes were pleading as much as his words.

I hesitated for one moment. Tyler might be upset with me, but I believed Sam. "Sure. Why don't you follow me?"

Sam went around back to the alley where he parked and met me at the corner intersection. I had given him the address in case we became separated, but I drove slow and kept my eye on the rearview mirror.

We pulled in front of the house, and I paused. A small house with four occupants limited privacy.

"Give me a minute, Sam."

I made a quick call to the café and got the OK from Stella before taking Sam into her home.

"Hey, Tyler. Can you come up here?"

He took the stairs two at a time.

"Pete fell asleep, and I thought it would be OK to leave him for a half hour. D.J.'s been with him."

"No problem. I need you to go over to Stella's"

"Sure. What for?"

I better tell him. I didn't need any more reasons to upset him. "Ty, I've been in touch with your dad. He wants to see you."

He took a step backward and sucked in his cheeks, all defenses up.

"I told you I didn't want to do that."

"I had to know, Ty. I couldn't believe he'd leave you. Do you know he spent years looking? He went back for you, like he said he would."

"You sure about that?"

"Very sure. Go see him, Ty. He's waited a long time."

Tyler paced for a moment. He looked like a scared kid. "Will you walk over with me?"

"Why?"

"I don't know. It feels kinda funny walking in and saying hi like nothing happened."

I patted his back. "OK, buddy. Let's go."

We walked over to Stella's. I opened the door, stepping aside to let Tyler walk in. He hesitated, but when Sam saw him, he bolted toward the door and scooped Tyler into his strong arms.

"Ty. Ty. I can't believe it." His voice cracked with emotion. "Ty, I'm so sorry. So sorry. I tried to find you."

I closed the door and left them to their reunion. Well, one piece of the puzzle worked out. It struck me that it was a big jigsaw puzzle. Matching pieces. Moving them around. Finding fits. I never saw that coming when I dreamed up this project.

I could only hope D.J. would share the same success. Those problems were an ocean deep.

30

Scott Harrington

Tyler and Sam spent three hours at Stella's house. I took them coffee after an hour, mostly to make sure the reconciliation was going well. I found them relaxed and catching up on nine missed years. Sam stopped in to say good-bye, and Tyler showed no signs of leaving with him.

"I'm going to stay here to help with Pete. When he's gone, I'll move in with my dad."

"Only if you want to. You have a place here if you ever need it."

"Thanks, Scott. But I belong with my dad. We have a lot of years to make up for."

"That's true. He seems like a good man."

"He's married again, and I have a sister. Her name's Laurel, and she's six years old. And, he's going to pay for me to go to college. He said money's not an issue. He told me business has been good and he's thrifty. His savings can cover college. No loans, no grants, no work study."

"That's wonderful. That'll let you concentrate on studying, not partying, right?"

"You know me better. I'm not a party kind of guy." His eyes darted toward Pete's bedroom. "I've seen what alcohol can do to a person. Never again will I live on the streets."

"I'm proud of you, Ty."

He shuffled uncomfortably. "I need to bring up something else. Your documentary?"

"Yeah, did you read the part I left for you?"

"I did."

"And?"

"It's pretty good."

"And?"

He continued to shuffle uneasily. "I'll sign your paper."

"Awesome!"

"Scott, I'm signing it for one reason. You've been good to me. Good to Pete and D.J. And I don't think it's because of wanting to write about us. I think it's because you care about people."

"I care about you three."

"There're things in every family that are..." He seemed to search for the right word. "That are ugly. Those are the things that you keep close to your heart, not the things that you show the whole world. When you publish that, everyone in the world will know my mother's a drunk, who went from man to man, moving in with guys she barely knew."

"But this isn't about her. This is about you, a victim of a poor home life."

"You can't write about me without writing about her. Not much love lost, but it feels funny. I guess disloyal. And my dad—well he's so sorry he didn't take me with him from the beginning. He'll be embarrassed for all of the world to know how that turned out."

My excitement washed away. I didn't want to

embarrass Sam. Could I reword it enough to avoid that?

Tyler shifted then continued. "What if someone wrote an article and went national, one that talked about your childhood? Talked about your domineering father and your mother not acting like much of a mother, and what if it talked about Edwin falling in with the wrong crowd and how he OD'ed under the bleachers. How would that feel for the whole world to know?"

My throat tightened, and I struggled to get a breath. Tyler sat with his elbow on the table, his head down and propped on his hand, the profile of *The Thinker*, as quiet as that mass of bronze. Silence hung between us. I stood and walked toward the stairs but did an about face, came up behind Tyler, and ruffled his hair. I couldn't be upset with him for speaking truth.

The doorbell rang, and Tyler answered it to let in the hospice nurse.

Shelving my concerns about the documentary. I pulled out the chart that we kept for logging medication and what he ate. "He hasn't been getting out of bed," I told her, "and he never wants to eat anything."

"I'll go check on him."

I walked her up the stairway and listened in while she examined Pete. He whispered when she asked about his pain level.

"OK, Pete. I'm going to check your pulse and blood pressure, temperature, and IV line."

After she was finished, we went back downstairs and gathered at the dining room table while she gave details about what the next forty-eight hours would look like.

There would be no Thanksgiving dinner for Pete. No reunion with his daughter. Just the final breaths from a jolly man with a gift for making people laugh.

31

Scott Harrington

The clock said 4:30 AM. as I slid in and out of sleep. Something felt wrong, and I couldn't place it. A tangible quiet hovered over the house without the peaceful sense that often accompanies silence. Pete. That's what I didn't hear. I jolted out of bed.

I hadn't heard Pete coughing or any raspy noises. When I opened the door to his room, D.J. was sitting beside the bed.

D.J. looked at me and answered my unspoken question with a shake of his head. "He's gone."

Old Pete had breathed his last on this side of heaven. It was a profound loss, even with the short time I knew him. How deep the loss must be for D.J. Grief had become his constant companion.

There's an awkwardness for men that women don't experience. Men don't hug or cry or talk about hurting. I put my hand on D.J.'s shoulder, an unspoken acknowledgment of the loss.

Did he sit here all night, somehow knowing?

"Why don't you get some sleep? I'll call hospice."

When D.J. left the room, I stood over the body of Pete Simmons. His was not a wasted life. Yes, I'd heard the hardships from his daughter. I'd heard of the hurt he inflicted...and it was wrong. If only she could have known old Pete in these last months. He'd been a rich storyteller, a man filled with laughter, eyes shining like they had some amusing secret. The normal life hadn't worked for Pete, but he'd carved out his own contentment. And he'd left a mark.

I eased the door closed and walked to the kitchen. Hospice would see to the arrangements since he had no family. He would be cremated and buried in a pauper's grave while four people mourned at his graveside.

I sat down to wait for the ambulance that would transport Pete to the morgue. There on the table lay the waiver Tyler had signed. I stared at it for the longest time without picking it up. Such a good kid. He signed that for me, despite the cost. Once so coveted, it now radiated heat like a brimstone, carrying the acrid smell of sulfur.

I moved to the kitchen and set up the coffee, ignoring the paper that mocked me from the center of the table. The transport arrived at seven thirty, without any fanfare, but the movement in the house pulled Tyler and D.J. from their beds. D.J. needed to be awake. He'd have a visitor today.

By eight, Pete's body had been taken from us. D.J. had gone to take a shower, possibly planning his return to the city. Stella arrived with her bag full of breakfast foods. Bagels, muffins, and fresh fruit filled the table. I helped her set plates and silverware when the doorbell suddenly rang at eight thirty.

I told Claire nine o'clock. D.J. hadn't come out yet after his shower. I answered the door, planning to suggest she give us fifteen more minutes.

But it wasn't Claire standing at the door. Mary

Anne Marshall, Pete's daughter, stood before me. Her eyes looked fatigued like she could use a good night's sleep.

"I hope it was OK to stop in."

"Of course. Come in." Had she somehow received the news? I waited, saying nothing.

"It's been a hard few weeks with everything happening at home and thinking about my father. My daughter had her baby last night. They're doing well. But being there. Seeing the miracle of new life. It seemed to make this whole thing with my dad a little easier. I knew last night I needed to come and see him."

The silence was deafening. We had been standing when she came and hadn't yet taken a seat. Tyler and Stella stood there with me. I knew I had to say something.

"Mary Anne, I'm so sorry, but it's too late. Pete's gone."

She covered her face and a gruff cry escaped. Stella grabbed a chair and placed it near her, leading her into it. She pulled another to the entry and motioned for me to sit. They left me to deal with an unexpected grief. Did it default to me because it was my house? Stella would have done better.

"Mary Anne, I'm so sorry. Can I get anything for you? Water or coffee?"

"No. Thank you. When did it happen?"

"He died during the night. They left a little while ago to take his body to the morgue."

"One day sooner. Why didn't I come sooner?" She talked to herself but looked up at me. "I'll be going now."

"Do you need someone to drive you?"

"No, I'm OK. I...I didn't think I'd be too late." I walked outside with her, trying to assess her ability to drive. She seemed to recover from the shock.

"Scott, thank you for doing what I should have done. I'm glad my father didn't die alone."

I nodded and gave her a side-shoulder hug. Then, she got back in her car and drove away. Old Pete would have been so happy to see her. I could almost hear him saying, "Well howdie do, Missy. Ain't you a sight for these sore ol' eyes."

But it was too late. Mary Anne had missed the opportunity to reconcile with her father. There's a point in time when there are no more chances.

With barely enough time to catch my breath, I prepared for the next visitor. Claire Bassett would arrive in ten minutes.

Stella, Tyler, and I agreed. When Claire arrived, as much as I would love to be an invisible eavesdropper, we would all move over to Stella's house.

D.J. came out of his room, cleaned and dressed. Yet my eyes were sharp and trained to observe. The cheeks still deepened, producing a gaunt, atrophied look to his face, a young man in an old body, draped in a blanket of sadness.

He took his coffee, sat in an easy chair, and flipped through a magazine and read one of my articles. I watched the window until Claire's car pulled in the driveway and parked in front of the house.

Without notice, Stella and Tyler stole away through the back door, and I went to the front, stepping outside.

Claire's cheeks held a rosy blush from the cold, and her eyes widened with apprehension. I squeezed reassurance into her mittened hand.

"He's in the living room, to your left when you enter. Is there anything I can do for you?"

She shook her head.

I motioned to Stella's house. "I'll be next door when you need me."

32

Claire Bassett

Closing the door behind me, I took a small step to see past the entry wall into the room where he sat. At first glance, I feared there had been a mistake. I saw a man seated there, thin, older, streaked with gray. The receding hairline and hollow look to his face did not belong to the husband I had known.

But it was Andrew. I silenced the cry that tried to leave my mouth. Breath caught in my throat, and I forced myself to inhale and exhale. I had waited so long for this moment.

His eyes buried in a magazine, he had not yet seen me, allowing me time to take a deeper look. There were the features I knew so well, hidden in this stranger. As I took a small step into the room, he looked up.

Neither of us spoke but stared as if seeing a mirage. He stood and took a few hesitant steps toward me. I stepped into the room and met him.

"Claire." It was a whispered plea.

I raised my hand to touch his face, feeling weathered skin, protruding cheekbones. I brushed a fallen lock of damp hair back from his forehead, unaware of my tears until his fingers found them, absorbing the dampness from my cheek. I hadn't spoken, but he continued whispering my name over and over.

Andrew's arms wrapped around me, drawing me to him. I rested my head against my husband's shoulder, his cheek pressing into me.

"I'm so sorry. I'm sorry." His sobs came, my hand circling his back, trying to still the racking that consumed him. Only once before did he weep in my embrace—the day of Ellory's death.

We held each other until we both cried ourselves out.

I inhaled, remembering the scent of him, my fingers spread wide over the cotton of his T-shirt. He buried his face against my shoulder. I moved my hand to his hair, holding him there, never wanting him to pull away.

He stepped back to cup my face, and he kissed me tenderly. We moved to the chair where he had been seated, and I slid onto his lap.

A year's worth of pent-up emotions collided inside of me, and I didn't know what to do with them.

"Why, Andrew? Why would you leave me?"

Instead of answering my question, his tears returned. He lowered his head into his hand. "Claire, I think I need help."

"You needed help then. Why did you have to leave?" I wanted to speak love to him, but I ached to have answers.

"The guilt was so huge, I couldn't see anything that would help me but punishment."

Were we still here? Still having this year-old discussion? "But it was an accident."

Andrew took my hands in his. "It was my fault."

"No, Andrew. You weren't held responsible. The investigation found you faultless."

He shook his head and squeezed my hand. "I'm not faultless."

"Honey, you are. It could have happened to anybody. Ellory ran behind you."

Andrew flinched at the sound of her name, pain visible in his eyes. His hands rubbed his head, and he held it as it sagged to his chest. His next words came so soft they were almost imperceptible. "While I was reading a text message."

My mouth opened, and I tried to look into his eyes, but he refused to look at me. Had I heard him correctly? "What did you say?"

He made eye contact with me and spoke with clarity. "I heard a text message come in and reached for my phone. I was in my driveway. I glanced to read it while I was backing out."

My throat burned with nausea. "Oh, Andrew, you never told me."

"I never told anyone. They never asked for my phone, and I never offered it."

"Oh, Andrew." I held him.

"I was in my driveway," he repeated.

A few minutes passed before either of us spoke again.

"Claire, I'm trying to do what needed to be done. The legal system had no justice, so I punished myself. I had to."

I moved and sat on the ottoman facing him. "Why?"

"I couldn't forgive myself. There was too much guilt."

I tipped his chin so he'd look at me. "What did that accomplish? Have you forgotten everything you once believed?"

"God forgives. I know that. But there had to be a consequence."

I stood again and paced. "Why, Andrew?"

"How could I go on and be happy like nothing happened? That isn't the way it should work."

I sat down on the ottoman again, taking his hand in mine, and softened my voice to counter the bluntness of my words. "Could you make atonement by punishing yourself? That was already done for you. Don't diminish the cross by living in false humility."

Andrew's eyes widened, and his mouth gaped open. He started to speak but was stopped by a cry in his words. His eyes darted to the Bible on the table beside him. Closing his eyes, he whispered a prayer. "God forgive me. Is that what I was doing?"

A spark of hope filled me for the first time since that awful day.

Andrew opened his eyes and turned them toward me. "My guilt and confusion squeezed out the truth. It felt way too simple for the weight of what I'd done."

"The beauty of the gospel is in its simplicity."

Andrew leaned forward and captured my hand in his. "Claire, I've made such a mess of things. Would you take me back after all this?"

My hesitation stunned me. I had cried and prayed and searched, longing for this very moment. Though I felt the beginning of hope, I still stared at a year's worth of rejection, the pain of being abandoned.

"Why didn't you come to me? Why did it have to be me looking for you?"

He rested his head on the chair. "I figured you moved on—wouldn't want me back after so long." He studied me, presumably appraising my expression to see if his statement held any truth. Jonathan's face flashed before me, a yoke of guilt.

"I've been looking for you for a year. I love you, and I want you back—want our family back. I know you've suffered, but I've suffered, too. You left me, left our children. I need to know what's going to happen now. I can't live every day wondering if you'll take off again."

Andrew sat forward, elbows on his knees, his chin resting on his hands. "It was never you. I tried to run from myself, but I guess that doesn't work. Grief doesn't go away, but it does fade. I still grieve over what happened, and I still feel guilt. But it's not the same intensity. It's a numb grief."

"We'd still have to have counseling, Andrew. There's too much hurt for us to deal with alone."

"I know. I guess I've left us in a financial mess."

"We can't think about that now. Counseling has to come first if we're going to get past this."

He reached and took my hand and his eyes reflected a lifetime of pain. "Claire, can you ever forgive me?"

I reached forward and stroked his cheek. Then I leaned in and placed my lips on his. "I forgave you long ago. That doesn't erase the hurt. I need to know you'll never leave me again."

"If you'll have me back, I'll do everything I can to make things right."

I needed an answer to my question. "I need to hear the words. Tell me you'll never leave me."

"I promise, I'll never leave you again. Never."

The tension left my face, my mouth forming the start of a smile. "Then please come home, Andrew. We've missed you."

He drew me toward him, holding me again.

There was a soft knock at the door, and we pulled apart. Scott poked his head around the wall.

"Everything all right here?"

We both nodded. Scott nodded, too. "Well, I'll just head on back next door."

And he softly clicked the door closed.

33

Scott Harrington

Ginger hopped onto the sofa and curled her body into a space smaller than she should have fit. With the lights dimmed, the small Christmas tree in the corner threw a pattern of stars on the ceiling. I hadn't planned on a tree, but Stella wouldn't hear of it. She came toting a disheveled four-foot pine.

"It's sad and needed a home. I happen to know this place opens its doors to the downtrodden."

We got a tree after all, Ginger and me. The dog rested her head on my lap as I stroked her rich brown fur.

"Just you and me, girl. Things are back to being quiet around here."

She responded with a satisfied sigh. I should have shared her contentment, but it wouldn't come. I looked at my laptop on the table before me. Everything was completed and written well. Sometimes I would re-read my work in progress and question its worth. But on a rare occasion, I would look at it and know I'd hit a home run. It would be picked up for publication by a high-end journal. A good chance of at least a Peabody, possibly even the Pulitzer. But it sat there waiting to be submitted. D.J, my third bio, didn't even know I'd used his story. I'd picked up the phone a few times to call but couldn't do it. They had suffered so much that it held me in check.

Stella's voice broke through my melancholy. She stuck her head in the door and called, "Anybody home?"

"In here, Stel."

"Hey, Mr. Fix-it. You made that tree look respectable. What's your next big project to restore?" She set a tray of Christmas cookies on my table.

"Only me."

"So, what's up with you?" She continued to unwrap the tray and rearrange the cookies that had shifted.

I should have stood up and walked to the table, but that would've required too much energy. "I'm still struggling with this documentary."

She turned surprised eyes my way. "I thought you said you finished it."

"I did."

"And so?" Realizing I wasn't coming over for her cookies, she carried the rearranged tray and set it on the coffee table before me.

I shook my head. "I don't know. Something doesn't feel right."

Stella pulled a chair close, her unblinking eyes scrutinizing me. "What doesn't feel right?"

I laughed without humor. "I think I succeeded. I wanted to make three people come alive and they did. Not from what I wrote, but from who they are. They aren't empty faces that my words brought to life. They're real people. They gave life to my words."

"Very poignant! You could turn poet."

"You poking fun at me?" I half grinned.

"Never. So, what do you think you'll do?"

"I haven't a clue. Do you have any sage advice?"

"Here's my advice. It's never the wrong decision to do the right thing."

I squinted one eye. "So...what's the right thing?"

"Hey, I'm a cook. That's for you to decide. Here. Have a cookie."

I reached for a little chocolate fudge drop and popped it in my mouth. "You've gotten to be so much like Pete—vague answers that tell me nothing."

"Like Pete? I'll take that as a compliment. Well, while you're sitting here clueless, are you planning to go home for Christmas?"

I sipped my water to counter the sweetness of the fudge. "I am home."

"You know what I mean. Are you going to see either of your parents?"

"Nope. Not enough accomplishments yet. I'll need another hundred years for that."

She turned solemn. "Scott, don't you think they'd want to see you?"

"Stel, seriously, this is how it is. If they see me, they'll be happy, or at least cordial. If they don't see me, they won't take notice. If I go to my dad's, a little way into the visit, he'll start pumping me full of questions to see what I'm doing with my life."

"And you can tell him how you alone helped three people out of their awful situations, set two of them on a path to success. That's significant."

I shook my head. "Not to Charles Harrington. It doesn't pad my bank account, and it doesn't give me infamous recognition."

She leaned forward, unblinking. "Do those things matter to you?"

"Not in the least."

"So what's the problem here?"

It took a while to put it into words.

"I guess I look at the others, at Tyler and D.J. They've got full lives now. D.J.'s getting help, they're moving to a fresh location, he has a new job."

"Yeah, I heard you say that. I don't suppose you had anything to do with that?"

I smiled. "I may have made a few connections."

"Mr. Fix-it."

"Tyler, well he's getting to know his stepmother and sister, looking forward to school. He's got so much ahead of him. I guess I feel like my world's a little empty."

Stella moved from her chair and shooed a reluctant Ginger to the floor, taking her spot on the sofa.

"So, why don't you fill it up? Get someone to share it with."

"That never seems to work for me."

She swiveled to face me, reached for my hand, and stroked the top of it. Her eyes stayed fastened on our joined hands before entwining our fingers. The warmth of her closeness always had a way of calming me.

Stella lifted her eyes. "Scott, sometimes what you want is right in front of you, so close you can't even see it."

She had said something similar not too long ago. Her eyes never left mine, they drilled me with softness. I'm slow at comprehending, but did she mean what I thought? I felt her hand in mine, soft and warm. I took in the features of her face, the fairness of her skin and smooth complexion, the blond hair matching light brows and blue eyes. Why had I never noticed they were blue? I searched her eyes, needing to understand.

For someone good with words, I managed to say the stupidest thing. "When did your eyes get so blue?"

The sides of her mouth lifted in a grin. "Oh, probably when I was three weeks old?" She shifted closer toward me. "Or maybe not until you really looked."

She reached and tapped my chin playfully. "When did you get that dimple in your chin?"

I smiled, which always accentuated the dimple, and gave her back her own answer. "Maybe when you first noticed."

Her hand lingered, soft and radiating warmth.

"Oh, I noticed. I noticed a long time ago."

Her eyes never left mine. We moved forward together, brushing our lips, testing each other's meaning. They were soft against mine, her lipstick releasing the spicy taste of cinnamon. How appropriate for Stella. I kissed her again, longer and deeper, loving the feel of her in my arms. How had I missed this? I whispered her name against her ear, a whisper filled with questions and hope. And she responded, her arms embracing me and her lips tracing my cheek.

When we pulled apart, this journalist had no words.

But Stella was never short of them. "It took you long enough, Harrington."

I regained my composure, and my heart flooded with emotion—Stella, Tyler's words, the documentary. I didn't make a snap decision born of a moment of passion. Instead I followed some wise advice. It's never a wrong decision to do the right thing.

I picked up Tyler's waiver that waited on the

coffee table before me and skimmed it one last time. Walking over to the fireplace, I fed the paper to the smoldering logs. It didn't immediately catch, giving me a momentary panic to retrieve it before the flames curled and blackened the words. Then the spark roared to life and it was no more.

Stella watched as I walked back to the sofa. I reached forward to the coffee table and touched my laptop to life. With deliberateness, I pulled up the file and found the key I wanted, and I pushed it without regret. Delete.

She motioned to the remaining waiver with one eyebrow arched in question.

"Pete's. He wanted to be famous."

"But...the file?"

"I had each bio in a separate file before I merged them." I turned toward her with a grin. "And do you really think I don't have a backup?"

"And your plan is?"

"A simple piece. The Life of a Wild Weasel."

Turning back to Stella, I opened my arms. "Now, speaking of wild, where were we?"

Epilogue

Four Years Later
Claire Bassett

I stole another glimpse out the kitchen window to check on the kids. Isabella, Drew, and Laurel, Tyler's step sister, ran through the yard playing ball with Muffin, Laurel's little sheltie. When we had pulled up to the house, I was thankful to see a fenced yard. Both Andrew and I still experienced anxiety when there was a road or driveway near the children.

I moved to peek around the door into the playpen where Peter slept. Such a healing balm to our family. Maybe because he wasn't there before. He held no associations with that terrible day.

I wish I could have known Pete. Andrew talked of him every day for the first year. Despite his weakness for alcohol, he'd had enough wisdom to know what Andrew needed—whether to talk or to reflect. Andrew loved the old man. He filled the role of father or brother.

The reconciliation with Matthew contributed greatly to Andrew's healing. Making the trip to Harrisburg amplified our stress, but Andrew knew it had to be face-to-face. Matthew's slumped posture and lack of energy spoke of the grief he lived out daily. Yet he embraced Andrew, told him he knew it was an accident. We may never return to the close relationship we once had, but for now, it's enough.

Stella finished pulling the salads from the refrigerator. "Everyone OK? Peter still asleep?"

"He's zonked. He played himself out. Laurel was great with him. How old did Tyler say she is?"

"She's ten, almost eleven. She was around six when he first met her. It's so neat to see how she hangs around him. I think she likes having a big brother." Stella set the salad dish on the counter.

"Look at this salad! You're amazing. You brought way too much."

"Hey, it's what I do. I love a busy kitchen. Did I hear that you're doing some cooking for a crowd, volunteering every week to serve breakfast downtown?"

"Yeah, St. John's. They're providing a vital need for the underserved population. I enjoy going in and helping."

Stella arched her back and stretched.

"Why don't you sit for a while? Your ankles look like they're swollen. What's your due date?"

"August sixth. Two more months."

"Scott said you don't know if it's a boy or girl. Are you going to find out or wait until birth?"

"We've been having fun with the mystery, but we'll find out. We decided to ask when I have my next sonogram."

"And this is the first grandchild?"

"For Scott's family but not for mine. We have scads of little ones but they're scattered through Illinois and Ohio. Scott's parents are still somewhat self-absorbed, but we're hoping a baby might change that. At least Scott's made an effort. He's done what he can to build a bridge." Stella sat on the closest chair and stretched her legs. A playful grin extended over her face. "I thought his dad would have a coronary when he saw Scott driving a minivan."

That was hard for me to understand since my parents were so caring. Sometimes overboard, but only because they loved us. Their relationship with Andrew had returned quickly. "I guess we're only responsible for what we do, no matter how others respond."

Sam's wife, Jane, came in to say the DVD and chairs were all ready.

I turned toward her. "Jane, your daughter is a saint. She's so patient with Drew. She's not much older than Bella, but sisters don't always have tolerance for their little brothers."

"They're having fun, but I'm about to break that up. We're ready to eat."

Once everyone gathered together, we stood in a circle and joined hands. Tyler honored Andrew by asking that he say the blessing. His personality had returned in bits and pieces, bringing back the strong leader that we once knew. He grasped my hand and gave it an extra squeeze. It still brought a rush of comfort when my hand rested in his.

"Let's pray, and then we'll take our plates into the family room to watch the salutatorian's graduation speech." We all bowed our heads to give thanks. "Father, we give You thanks today for this reunion, such a reminder of Your goodness and grace. Thank You for the accomplishments that we celebrate today, for the strong, reliable man that Tyler has become, for the influence of his father. We give thanks for Scott's role in his life, in my life, and in Pete's. Thank You that we can all carry a little piece of Pete's kindness and contentment.

"Today, You have marked the beginning of a new path for Tyler, a new career in public service, and rewarded his efforts with recognition at the ceremony. We're all so proud to be part of his life. Please keep Your hand upon him that he may always walk in faith.

"Please bless this food and the hands that have prepared it."

Everyone said Amen. We took our seats, and Sam turned to speak to the small gathering.

"We wanted to invite each of you to the graduation, but our tickets were limited. We're glad that you can celebrate it with us tonight. And, I'm not bragging or anything, but I might add that one tenth of a percentage point separated the salutatorian and the valedictorian." He pushed start on the DVD. We watched as they introduced Tyler and as he approached the podium with confidence.

"My name is Tyler Pulkowski, and I'm standing here today on the shoulders of some significant people in my life, people who believed in me and sacrificed for me. I suspect every person present could make that statement. Whose shoulders are you standing on? We aren't designed to live in isolation. We're designed to need people. Every life will have high points and low points, and sometimes the low points look hopeless. I've been there, been to the bottom of all hope. But someone looked beyond himself, beyond his dreams, goals, and aspirations. He saw a need and he chose sacrifice.

My challenge to each person here today is this: dream and plan. Set goals and aim high. But never allow those to surpass human need. I was able to achieve this milestone in my life because another person set his goal aside. I want to honor that sacrifice by having eyes wide open to the needs of hurting people.

Today is the day we all begin a new chapter in life. Standing here in all of our regalia, a day of entitlement, of feeling that it's all about us. It isn't. It's all about those who enabled you to be here today. It's their accomplishment, their victory march. Your accomplishment comes when you rise to the challenge of looking beyond yourself. Ronald Reagan shared this thought with us. 'You can't help everyone, but everyone can help someone.' Go and find that someone."

The video finished and Tyler turned his head toward Scott. One by one, Andrew, Sam, and I each glanced in that direction. Stella slid her hand into his. Where would we be today if he hadn't looked beyond himself? The words of scripture sprang to my mind and I spoke them aloud. "The King will reply, 'Truly I tell you, whatever you did for one of the least of these brothers and sisters of mine, you did for Me."

A Devotional Moment

And the King will answer them, 'Truly, I say to you, as you did it to one of the least of these my brethren, you did it to me.' ~ Matthew 25:40

God has given the commandment that we are to help "the least of these" —widows, orphans, the homeless, those with physical or mental disabilities, those who have nothing, and those who don't have the means to take care of themselves. We are not to discriminate in any way, and we are not to exploit others for our own gain. This directive is sometimes difficult because the pressure from peers or the temptation for self-gain is great. But God tells us that how we treat others is considered as treating Jesus in the same way. Respect and consideration is the correct path, the path that leads us to God.

In **The Least of These**, the protagonist is in a situation where he will earn accolades and favor at the cost of other people's privacy. As he gathers information he is drawn into the stories of the men, and comes to understand that gossip hurts and sometimes secrets are meant to be kept.

Have you ever been in a situation where you've been tempted to harm someone's livelihood or reputation in order to elevate yourself? Maybe you justified the situation (they have enough already, or they have so little it won't affect them at all) or maybe you truly didn't realize the damage your actions would cause. Understand that how we treat others affects us more than it affects them. God knows our hearts, minds and motives; and judges accordingly.

LORD, TEACH ME NOT TO TURN A BLIND EYE TO THOSE IN NEED, BUT TO HELP AND MINISTER TO THEM FREELY SO THAT THEY MAY SEE THE LIGHT OF YOUR LOVE. HELP ME TO RESPECT THE RIGHTS OF ALL HUMAN BEINGS NO MATTER THEIR STATUS OR MINE. IN JESUS' NAME I PRAY, AMEN.

Acknowledgements

Although writing may be a solitary activity, the road to publication is not. Many hands have contributed to this work of fiction. First, I want to give my heartfelt thanks to my husband, Vaughn Neely. He encourages me and enables me to write. Thank you to my son, Stephen Neely, for fine tuning the details of my Pittsburgh landmarks.

I'd like to express my gratitude to my writing group, Cross N Pens. It's a joy to partner with you. Thank you, Cynthia Owens and Tim Suddeth for your careful editing and helpful suggestions. You believed I could do this even when I wasn't convinced.

When the first draft was completed and I sought an early reader, I knew I'd have to call Linda Smith, the most avid reader I know. When I'm looking for a book to read, I seek her reviews because they'll be spot on. Thank you, Linda, for being my first audience, for offering effective feedback, and for your encouraging words.

I am grateful to Pelican Book Group and delighted to be part of their network of authors. They are a delightful group. A very special thanks goes to Megan Lee for her skillful editing. I'm so grateful for your expert help.

Above all, I thank God for the privilege of writing. May He be forever praised.

Thank you...

for purchasing this Harbourlight title. For other inspirational stories, please visit our on-line bookstore at www.pelicanbookgroup.com.

For questions or more information, contact us at customer@pelicanbookgroup.com.

Harbourlight Books
The Beacon in Christian Fiction™
an imprint of Pelican Book Group
www.pelicanbookgroup.com

Connect with Us
www.facebook.com/Pelicanbookgroup
www.twitter.com/pelicanbookgrp

To receive news and specials, subscribe to our bulletin
http://pelink.us/bulletin

May God's glory shine through
this inspirational work of fiction.

AMDG

You Can Help!

At Pelican Book Group it is our mission to entertain readers with fiction that uplifts the Gospel. It is our privilege to spend time with you awhile as you read our stories.

We believe you can help us to bring Christ into the lives of people across the globe. And you don't have to open your wallet or even leave your house!

Here are 3 simple things you can do to help us bring illuminating fiction™ to people everywhere.

1) If you enjoyed this book, write a positive review. Post it at online retailers and websites where readers gather. And share your review with us at reviews@pelicanbookgroup.com (this does give us permission to reprint your review in whole or in part.)

2) If you enjoyed this book, recommend it to a friend in person, at a book club or on social media.

3) If you have suggestions on how we can improve or expand our selection, let us know. We value your opinion. Use the contact form on our web site or e-mail us at customer@pelicanbookgroup.com

God Can Help!

Are you in need? The Almighty can do great things for you. Holy is His Name! He has mercy in every generation. He can lift up the lowly and accomplish all things. Reach out today.

Do not fear: I am with you; do not be anxious: I am your God. I will strengthen you, I will help you, I will uphold you with my victorious right hand.

~Isaiah 41:10 (NAB)

We pray daily, and we especially pray for everyone connected to Pelican Book Group—that includes you! If you have a specific need, we welcome the opportunity to pray for you. Share your needs or praise reports at http://pelink.us/pray4us

Free Book Offer

We're looking for booklovers like you to partner with us! Join our team of influencers today and periodically receive free eBooks and exclusive offers.

For more information
Visit http://pelicanbookgroup.com/booklovers